Caro gaz

"This could be a pattern killer," she said.

"This could be a major crime scene," Mike said. "And you're a civilian. You shouldn't be here."

"I'm co-owner of a psychological counseling center," Caro answered, sounding as cool as he did skeptical. "Police often consult us in the case of pattern killings."

"Look, Caro," Mike said. "I really can't talk now. How about getting together later?"

"I can see you're busy," she said. "Unfortunately, I think I'm going to be just as busy later."

Before he could answer, she was headed down the embankment, keeping her head admirably straight. Was he letting his only chance get away? What if she *could* profile the killer for him?

He watched her traverse the bottom of the incline. Dapples of sunlight caught the reddish glints in her hair, and Mike felt each one like a spark in his heart.

ABOUT THE AUTHOR

Alice Orr grew up in the small city of Watertown, New York, where this story is set. She now lives in the big City of New York. She has learned that both places, like the past and the present, have an up side and a down—but you can only live in today. She shares that here-and-now life with her husband, Jonathan, and the fifty-some clients of the Alice Orr Agency.

Books by Alice Harron Orr

HARLEQUIN INTRIGUE
 56–SABOTAGE
169–PAST SINS

Cold Summer

Alice Harron Orr

Harlequin Books

TORONTO • NEW YORK • LONDON
AMSTERDAM • PARIS • SYDNEY • HAMBURG
STOCKHOLM • ATHENS • TOKYO • MILAN
MADRID • WARSAW • BUDAPEST • AUCKLAND

To my husband, Jonathan—
always my romantic hero.

And to my son, Ed,
(who drew the map for this book
and for my previous Intrigue as well)—
he has always been there when I needed him.

Harlequin Intrigue edition published February 1993

ISBN 0-373-22216-5

COLD SUMMER

Printed in U.S.A.

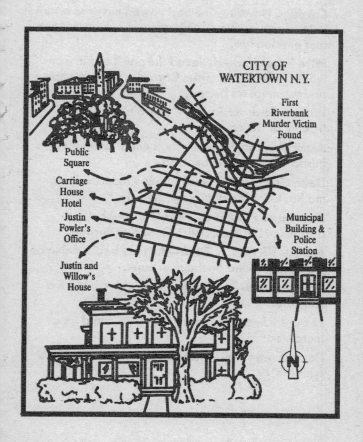

CAST OF CHARACTERS

Caroline Hardin—She had vowed never to return to the north country, but her friend was in danger and needed her.

Mike Schaeffer—He loved the north country and would never leave. Then Caro Hardin came home and the murders began.

Willow Gilchrist Fowler—She is either in big trouble or the cause of it.

Justin Bennett Fowler—He is either a devoted husband or a man obsessed.

Della Gilchrist—Willow's loving mom and the mother Caroline always wished she had.

Lieutenant Palumbo—Mike's wise-cracking partner at the local Police Detective Bureau.

Murder Victims 1, 2 & 3—All they had in common was being found on the riverbank.

Tim Manders—A troubled man who could be a murderer.

Lester Pickett—An angry man who could be a murderer.

Parnell Janeway—A fanatical man who could be a murderer.

Chapter One

To say Caroline Hardin was nervous about returning to her hometown would be an understatement. In fact, she was amazed she had managed the nearly four-hundred-mile drive without hyperventilating. Not a psychologically strong position for a would-be psychologist, but she couldn't help that. Years had passed since her last visit to northern New York State, and if it hadn't been for Willow Fowler's desperate pleas on the phone last night, Caroline wouldn't be here now.

Watertown, New York, might be the place she grew up in, but mostly she'd thought of it as the place she couldn't wait to get out of. As far back as she could remember, escaping the north country had been something of an obsession. She had that feeling again now, as she steered her yellow sports car off Washington Street.

She had turned her back on this town after graduating from high school and had come home only a very few times in the fifteen years since.

A thought struck her with such vivid intensity it might as well have been spelled out in letters several feet high on a billboard stretched across the road in front of her. She should have kept her promise to herself about not coming back here. This trip was a big mistake. She knew she should head back south to Westchester as fast as these eight cylinders and their considerable horsepower would allow.

Instead, she gunned the engine more emphatically than was either wise or necessary to traverse the hump in the driveway to the Holiday Inn parking lot. She wasn't going back anywhere. Not tonight anyway. She was bone tired and half-blind from staring at highway lines and approaching headlights. She might decide to make her retreat in the morning, but for now she had reached journey's end.

The arc of her own headlights darted across the expanse of empty lot adjoining this more populated one. She had clicked off the high beams when she left the main highway for the last leg of her trip north from Westchester. She reached to turn off her lights altogether just as their beam revealed a single car in the adjacent lot. A man was sitting inside with his hand on the open driver's side door. He glanced up quickly, then turned abruptly away and jerked the door shut.

How appropriate, Caroline thought. I left this town because people kept slamming doors in my face. I come back, and the first person I see does the same thing.

She smiled at her own sense of melodrama. After all, wasn't she returning home in triumph, her kit bag filled to the brim with both scholastic and professional accomplishments sure to wow the locals?

Except that they wouldn't be wowed, of course. She had tried that approach on a couple of previous visits. She had been determined to prove to every single soul north of Syracuse how badly they had under-estimated her and how much they had missed out on when they drove her away from here. Unfortunately, her hometown girl makes good routine had been a to-tal flop. The only response she got was some advice to get the chip off her shoulder. She hoped she would know enough not to try that again.

What she really ought to do was thank each and every individual in this town who ever gave her a hard time when she was growing up. Without them, she might never have flown the nest, might never have found her way to those accomplishments in the first place.

Of course, her wings could use a rest once in a while. In fact, she was near exhaustion right now, as she dragged her lightweight parachute-cloth suiter bag from the passenger seat and crawled out of the low-slung car. She had promised herself she wasn't going to be too negative about coming back here. She shouldered the strap of the suiter and adjusted her balance to support its bulk before heading around to the back of the car.

As usual, she had packed too much. Economy of expression might be her forte on the fund-raising cir-cuit. Economy of luggage was not, especially not for this trip. She might have resolved not to toot her own horn professionally while she was here in the north-land, that didn't mean she couldn't dazzle the coun-tryside with sophisticated chic.

Caroline sighed again into a night that was chilly for July. She had carried a lot more baggage up here than this practical matched set. She had also lugged along the stuff she'd had tucked away in the attic of her psyche for all these years since she left Watertown for good. She had been aware of those long ignored items reattaching themselves, one by one, as she drove north. Now, as she approached the back door of the hotel, she could feel that psychic luggage weighing her down more heavily than any number of overstuffed carryalls.

Caroline used the smaller bag to nudge open the glass door into the rear lobby. A sign on the wall indicated the restaurant to her right down a wide hallway lined with blow-up photos of the town's earlier, lovelier days. There had been a drive-through in place of this corridor the last time Caroline stayed here.

It occurred to her that in their younger years, Willow would most likely have been waiting in the restaurant bar, surrounded by friends and admirers. Willow's bright, highly charged spirit drew people to her. That spirit occasionally lured the wrong species, but no real harm had ever come of it. Certainly nothing like the trouble Willow claimed to be in now.

There had been no mistaking Willow's fear as she begged Caroline to come up here, and, despite her reluctance, Caroline could hardly ignore the pleas of the woman who had been her first real friend in those difficult years of adolescence when a friend was what she needed most in the world.

Consequently, here she was, trundling two heavy bags to the registration desk and so self-absorbed that she nearly ran into the man standing stock-still in front of her. She looked up to apologize, but the words flew out of her mind before she could utter them.

The carryall slipped from her grasp, and the suiter might have done the same had its strap not been an-

chored behind the shoulder pad of her fashionable
linen jacket. In one of those incongruous flashes of
thought that can happen in a moment of shock, she
wished she hadn't worn linen, no matter how fashionable. She must look like one big wrinkle right now,
and that was hardly the image she wanted to present
the first time she saw Mike Schaeffer again.

Over the past several years, if you had asked Caroline about Mike Schaeffer, she would have said she'd
all but forgotten him and believed that to be true. Now
she was discovering that she remembered him all too
well. She stared up into his face, and suddenly she was
fourteen years old again, filled with the confusing,
exciting, wonderful, terrible feelings he had aroused
in her even then. Four hundred miles ago she might
have been a savvy, professional woman who could
maintain her cool under any circumstances, but here
on this spot she was once more a north country girl
with an aching adolescent crush on somebody way out
of her reach.

MIKE COULD HARDLY believe his eyes. Caroline Hardin, all grown up, practically walking into his arms.
The last time that had happened she had been maybe
thirteen or fourteen to his twenty-two going on ancient.

He'd been fresh back from Nam and thought of
himself as pretty worldly-wise about women and just
about everything else. Even so, what had happened
that night had affected him so strongly that he'd
known he must keep his distance from Caro Hardin.
She was a kid after all, and he was a grown man, a war
veteran. He'd seen men die. He'd seen a lot of things.

Yet even as he'd told himself he had to stay away from her, he'd known that he had never seen anything as lovely as Caro standing in his bedroom doorway with the hall light behind her, haloing her hair.

He had stayed away from her all the same, all through her high school years. And then she had gone off to college never to return to Watertown. He supposed there had been something about her that was beyond the north country. Looking at her now, he could tell that was more true than ever. He was startled by the intense pang of disappointment that realization made him feel.

"Mike, how are you?" she asked finally, and the sound of her voice made his heart skip.

"I can hardly believe it's you, Caro," he said, using the old nickname he'd given her years ago. "I was sure you'd never come back here."

"Oh, I've passed through a few times, but never for more than a day or so." She shifted the shoulder strap of the bag she was carrying.

"Let me take those for you."

Mike eased the wide webbed strap out from under the soft fullness of her dark hair; the brush of it tingled the back of his hand as if he'd touched something electric. As he bent to pick up her other bag he caught the tantalizing scent of some exotic, no doubt expensive, cologne.

"Watertown still isn't big enough to merit bellboys," he said.

"I can generally manage on my own."

"Yes, I'd expect that of you."

She'd always had an independent streak, even as a kid. He guessed that's how she had dared to come into his room that night. Mike remembered it as if it were yesterday, her standing in the doorway with her dark curls falling over the collar of her girlish robe. He also remembered that, for all her boldness, she'd been trembling.

"Are you just passing through again, or are you planning to stay awhile?" he asked, hoping she hadn't heard the catch in his voice prompted by his memories.

"I'll probably be here a few days at least."

"If I'd known you were coming, I would have ordered some warm sunshine. This summer's been real cold so far."

Mike nearly groaned out loud. He couldn't believe he was talking about the weather!

"This isn't a vacation," she said, but she didn't go on to explain what her mission was.

"Well, any time you need an official toter and carrier, just give me a holler." She had walked to the registration counter as they talked, and he set her bags down in front of it. "In fact, I'll carry these to your room for you once you check in."

"Thanks," she said quickly, "but I'll manage."

Her smile was polite but not what he would call friendly. Doubtless he was making a fool of himself, all because of the power of something that had happened in the dim and distant past. The chances that this beautiful woman even remembered an obscure incident back when she was a teenager were slim to none.

"Okay," he said with a polite smile of his own. "Maybe we'll run into each other again before you leave town. If not, enjoy your visit."

"Thanks," she said, and her cool facade seemed to waver for an instant.

Then she was cool and composed once more—and obviously eager to be rid of him. So he simply nodded and walked away toward the restaurant, where he'd been headed in the first place—though at the moment he couldn't remember why he was going there, or much else either for that matter.

CAROLINE ATTEMPTED to concentrate on the room registration until she could be certain Mike was out of sight. Then she let herself exhale fully for the first time since she'd looked up into those serious gray eyes of his. Damn. She had signed her name on the wrong line of the registration card.

For some reason, Mike Schaeffer had always brought out the silly fool in her.

The first time she ever saw him, he had just come back from Vietnam. She'd been curious about that, what it must have been like to be somewhere you got shot at and had to shoot back, maybe even kill people. She had wanted very much to get to know him. She brought that about by befriending his sister who always needed help with her English homework, while Caroline had straight A's. That was how she first actually met Mike, and her infatuation began. By the time she wangled that fateful invitation to stay overnight at the Schaeffers', Caro Hardin was already hopelessly in love, or as much so as a girl can be at fourteen.

She felt her cheeks warm at the memory and grabbed her room key card from the counter before the hotel clerk could see her blush. She had committed the ultimate teenage transgression that night: she had thrown herself at a man who could hardly have been less interested in her. Nothing had come of it, of course, and he had been gracious enough not to laugh in her face. Still, she could well remember the humiliation she'd felt.

She wasn't quite sure what she had been after when she snuck into his room once Judy fell asleep—she had probably thought they would neck for a while—but Caroline definitely hadn't expected that he would ask her to leave. But after one kiss—which had been her doing, not his—that's exactly what he had done. And quite firmly.

Caroline grabbed her bags and hefted them toward the short flight of steps leading to the first-floor wing where her room was located. Her cheeks were flaming now. She had to get out of this lobby before somebody came along to witness her emotional disarray—all because of the memory of a long-ago kiss. But what a kiss it had been! Every kiss after had been measured against that night and found wanting. She hadn't really understood that until this moment, but now there could be no denying the fact that she was as infatuated with Mike Schaeffer as ever. This time, however, she would make certain he didn't find out.

She had handled their meeting well, she reminded herself. She had kept cool and impersonal despite the fact that his voice, with its occasional, endearing crack and rasp, made her remember how much she once yearned to have him sing her a folk love ballad with a soft guitar behind it. They were only a couple of years out of the sixties and she'd been a very young girl, so such fantasies were acceptable if not wise. However, she was no longer a lost and lonely fourteen-year-old girl, and would do well to remember that.

She was repeating that resolve to herself and fitting her card into the lock on her hotel-room door when someone slipped up beside her. It was Willow, and she was carrying a suitcase.

"Get inside. Quickly!" Willow whispered.

Before Caroline could even register how surprised she was by this unusual greeting, Willow's long, delicate fingers with their perfectly shaped nails were flat against the door and pushing it open. She slid through the opening as quietly as she had whispered in Caroline's ear a moment before.

Caroline followed her inside and watched as her old friend dropped her suitcase and hurried to the wide windows that fronted on Washington Street. She pulled the drapes hastily shut, then peeked out through a crack among the folds.

"Please, shut the door," she said, urgency in her voice.

Caroline set her bags beside Willow's and closed the door as directed. She flipped the door guard shut as well with her usual urban paranoia that prompted her behavior at the moment. She had seen the look in Willow's eyes and something there had leapt, like contagion, across the room. Caroline found herself suddenly afraid and not liking the feeling one bit.

"What is going on here, Willow?"

"Caro, you have to believe me. I'm in real trouble."

"I believe you. I wouldn't be here otherwise."

"Oh, and I can't thank you enough for coming." Willow darted across the room to grasp Caroline's hand and pull her over to sit on the edge of one of the two double beds. "I was so afraid you wouldn't be able to drop everything and drive all this way just to help me out."

"I'm between projects right now, so I could manage it more easily than usual. Besides, I haven't forgotten that you were always there for me all those years ago."

"Be that as it may, I don't remember anybody doing anything half so kind for me—ever."

Caroline smiled. Willow had always used phrases like "Be that as it may." Sometimes she sounded like a little, old spinster lady with antimacassars on the arms of her chairs. Actually, however, Willow Gilchrist Fowler was anything but spinsterish. Her irrepressible vivacity was what had drawn Caroline to her in the first place. Caroline had had her own head of energetic steam in those days, driven by her resolve to get out of northern New York State and make something of herself. Still, there had been times when her mother's relentless criticism and her father's seeming indifference, coupled with a society so callous to her dreams, had threatened to bring Caroline down too far for rising up again.

Those were the moments when having Willow for a friend was such a special blessing. Caroline would plug into Willow's exuberance and before long feel recharged and ready to take on just about anybody if she had to.

Maybe she could repay some of that wealth of kindness and caring now, and that felt good. What didn't feel good was seeing the way Willow's usual liveliness had translated itself into a frazzled state of obvious panic.

"What exactly has Justin done to you anyway? I wasn't quite clear about that from our phone call," Caroline began.

Last night Willow had insisted she must get away from her husband, even if it took drastic measures to do so.

"I didn't tell you more because I was afraid you'd think I was exaggerating." Willow grabbed Caroline's hand again, then let go, as if she were grasping at hope but too agitated to hold on. "It's hard even for me to believe how he's taken over my life so completely. Everything about me, every move I make. Sometimes I think I don't really exist any longer— there's only him and his version of me left."

"He is your husband, Willow," Caroline soothed, "and sometimes husbands can be a bit possessive. That doesn't mean you have to be frightened of him, does it?"

"It's not like that!" Willow exclaimed. "You're talking about normal marriages, normal relationships. This isn't at all like that!" She clasped her hands and clutched them against her chest. "Glory be, what ever am I going to do?"

Caroline was reminded of her own occasional tendency toward melodrama. "Have you tried simply talking to him?"

"Of course, I have, but it doesn't work. Nothing works."

"What about going to a counselor, or someone who can mediate for you?"

"The only two therapists here in town are both his dear friends. Everybody's his dear friend. They all think he's the best thing that ever happened to the north country."

"But he's shown you a different side of himself than the others see—is that what you're saying?"

"Yes, yes, that's it," she said with a shudder.

Willow sounded near hysteria, and right now it was more important to calm her down than to verify the details of her fear of Justin.

"Everything's going to be all right," Caroline said gently as she pushed Willow's honey-brown hair back from her flushed cheeks. "We'll handle this together. But you're going to have to tell me something of what has happened."

"What happened is that I made a critical error in judgment in marrying Justin Fowler."

Saying his name seemed to make Willow more agitated than ever. She darted up from the bed and over to the dressing table, pacing nervously this way and that.

She was expensively dressed in a pale cream silk dress and matching jacket. Her soft leather pumps were the same cream color and of Italian design. Willow had always loved nice things, and since she married Justin, she'd had them in abundance. Her recent visits to Caroline had been mainly quick stops along the way to shopping forays in New York City, where Justin had opened accounts for Willow in some of the finest, priciest stores. Caroline remembered once when she had complimented Justin's generosity. Willow had passed it off as "an investment in his image." Caroline had wondered at the time if Willow wasn't being rather unappreciative.

Willow had spoken on the phone about needing to get away, and Caroline had offered to have her come for a visit while things cooled down with Justin. Willow had insisted she must make a more permanent escape, but she didn't know how to go about it.

"I want to help," Caroline said, "but you have to tell me more about what the problem seems to be."

"Well, first of all, he interrogates me every time I want to go out. And then, whenever I do get out, he follows me around or has me followed. He even goes through scraps of paper I've thrown away, looking for clues to things he thinks I haven't told him about my life! I used to have a job. It wasn't anything extraordinarily important, but I enjoyed it. Justin didn't want me to work, so he stayed home himself and held me prisoner in the house for several days and wouldn't let me call into the office. They fired me, of course. He said if I tried to tell anyone—as if anyone would believe me!—or if I didn't do what he told me to do, he would lock me up and throw away the key. Is that enough to make me want to get out of town, or would you care to hear more?"

She was pacing the floor, and her words were choked with tears and frustration. Caroline would have liked to tell her to sit down and try to be calm but doubted that would work. Meanwhile, she wondered if you really could snap people out of hysteria by slapping them across the face. She hoped she wouldn't have to find out.

"I want to hear whatever you want to tell me," she said.

"Justin caught me with somebody else. The guy had only driven me home from the unemployment office. I swear it. I'd gone there to check out job listings, hoping I might find something part-time that Justin wouldn't have to find out about. This fellow was one of the counselors. I was so upset, he offered me a ride home. All we did was talk about places I might find work. I had thought Justin was going out of town that day, but I was wrong. He made sure I paid for it, too."

Willow sat down on the other bed, her slender shoulders sagging.

"What did he do?" Caroline urged, hoping to keep Willow talking.

"First of all, he came out of the house bellowing like a crazy man. He tore open the car door and yanked me out as if I were a wayward child or a piece of baggage. He screamed at the poor fellow—Mark Perkins was his name—and told him that if he ever saw him hanging around me again he would beat him within an inch of his life. After Mark left, Justin told me that if he ever caught me with another man again, he would kill the both of us. He even showed me the gun he would use to do it."

Willow paused a moment, then spoke with the heaviness of resignation. "He makes certain I know that he knows everywhere I go, everywhere I've been. He lets me know—sometimes in subtle ways, sometimes not so subtle—that he can always find me, no matter how hard I try to get away from him." Her hand rose to her throat. "The man is suffocating the very life out of me."

Caroline could see the truth of those words in her friend's pale complexion and haunted eyes. Willow was wrong about one thing. Caroline did understand how terrible it would be to feel trapped, when nothing in the world mattered so much as finding a way out. That had been the way she felt too much of the time in the years before she left this town.

Caroline sat down on the bed and put her arms around Willow. She didn't pull away, but she also didn't yield entirely to being comforted. Willow simply sat there, with silent tears falling on her cream silk dress, while Caroline held her and tried her best to be the friend her friend deserved.

Chapter Two

Willow hunched forward, trying to find something in her purse by the dim glow of the dash lights.

"Let me turn on the overhead for you," Caroline said, reaching for the switch.

"No, don't!"

Willow grabbed Caroline's hand, startling her. Her other hand jarred the steering wheel unintentionally in response, and the fine-tuned sports car veered toward the shoulder of the road. The tires sprayed gravel before Caroline could correct the swerve.

"Pray, forgive me," Willow said, sounding every bit the damsel in distress of a nineteenth-century novel. "Turning that light on would make me too much of a target. And you, too, I'm afraid."

"A target for what?"

Caroline was more than willing to be here for her friend, as the psycho-babblers would put it. But that didn't necessarily include being run off the road because of a fit of hysteria.

"He's watching," Willow said in a nervous whisper. "He's always watching."

"This road is nearly deserted, Willow. We haven't seen five cars in the last five miles, and I'd notice if somebody was following us."

"Then maybe I really have escaped his clutches this time." Willow had continued fumbling in her bag as they talked. Now she pulled out a small plastic tube.

"Are you telling me that a prominent citizen like Justin is skulking around some back road looking for you? Somehow that doesn't seem to jibe with the Justin I've met."

Caroline's admittedly brief acquaintance with Justin Fowler had revealed a suave, sophisticated businessman whose preoccupation with his ambitious career pursuits would seem to preclude the time-consuming task of playing watchdog to his wife.

"He doesn't need to do such lackey's work himself," Willow said as she struggled with trembling hands to snap off the cap of the plastic tube.

Not for the first time that night did Caroline wish she had more psychology credentials under her belt. Though she'd studied it in college and to this day was pursuing courses toward full accreditation as a counselor, she had opted for an M.B.A. on her path to total independence. Her association with Dr. Helena Blanchard, as co-owners of a family therapy clinic back in Westchester, had put Caroline on the administration and promotion end of the business, and she enjoyed the challenge as well as the opportunity to consult with a talented psychologist on a daily basis. Until recently that role had been enough for her. Maybe it still was. But maybe a second reason for her trip up here today had been the impulse to reassess her goals.

Still, Caroline had gleaned a great many insights into both normal and abnormal psychology, and she hoped that those, coupled with her long-standing friendship with Willow, no matter how infrequently they had seen each other of late, would help out in this confusing and emotionally charged situation.

"What have you got there?" Caroline asked as Willow tipped several white disks out into her palm.

"Antacids," Willow said, popping them into her mouth. "You may have observed that I am a veritable bundle of nerves."

"I can see that."

Caroline tried to weigh whether or not Justin Fowler might truly have henchmen on his wife's trail. Willow was clearly a wreck, and Caroline was beginning to wonder just what she had gotten herself into here.

Suddenly, unbidden, as if out of the darkness of the highway, the image of Mike Schaeffer popped into Caroline's mind. He certainly had looked good, even better than he had all those years ago. Back then despite the troubled eyes and the tension around his mouth, his face had still been softened somewhat by youth. Now he had the visage of a man full grown, sharply honed with character and depth. And Caroline was certain that, beneath his clothes, his body had hardened into lines and muscles as attractive and interesting as those of his face.

That errant thought shocked her back to the present like an alert signal flashing in her brain. She had no business thinking such things about Mike Schaeffer. As far as she knew, he was a happily married man. That charge of tension she had felt in the air between them tonight could have been a figment of her own creation and probably was. And, speaking of over-active imaginations, she should be confining her attentions to Willow right now instead of indulging an adolescent fantasy exaggerated by an adult libido.

"Where exactly are we headed?" she asked, hoping to dispel the fantasy with the voice of reality.

"A friend of mine has a house out on the Burrville Road, just past the cider mill. Do you remember where that is?"

"I remember."

The smell of apples, strong and sweet, wafted through Caroline's memory. Early every fall the presses would set to work in the long wooden building on the bank of the creek where Burrville Falls sheeted down over their rock shelf with enough force to power the mill wheel in the old days. Electric generators did the job now, but Caroline was sure the falls still sheeted down, as dark green sleek and gleaming in the sun as ever.

She and Willow had been driving out Gotham Street Road for some time now, over the rounded hillocks and through the meandering turns that were typical of north country secondary roads. They were driving in the dark now, but Caroline could still visualize their surroundings. She had taken her bicycle along this road many times when she was in junior high school and pedaling all over the countryside had been a major means of escape for a few hours from her mother's critical voice.

Caroline remembered that the old reformatory was out this way.

Whenever she had stepped out of line as a kid, which was almost daily in her mother's estimation,

Mrs. Hardin would threaten to ship Caroline off to one of two places, the orphanage or the reform school. By the time she was old enough to be taking those long junior high school bicycle jaunts, she had figured out the emptiness of her mother's threats. Still, she could remember pedaling a little faster as she passed the once-dreaded institution.

Which reminded her of why she was here with Willow now. Junior High was where Willow and Caroline first met and became friends. Willow had guessed early on that there were problems at home for Caroline, or maybe she had heard talk about it. Caroline's family was big on keeping secrets, but that was hard to do in the north country. So, Willow had known and sympathized. She had offered the sanctuary of her own home any time Caroline needed it, and Caroline had taken her up on it. She had spent a lot of time at the house on St. Mary Street with Willow and her sometimes scatterbrained but always sweet mother, Della Gilchrist. That was why there had been no choice but to respond to last night's frantic phone call from Willow. Caroline was only chipping away at a very sizable debt by doing so.

Speaking of frantic, Willow appeared to be moving in that direction right now. The antacids might have calmed her stomach, but they hadn't done a thing for her nerves. She was shaking the tablet cylinder back and forth, back and forth, rattling the contents from one end to the other with a sound that threatened to get on Caroline's nerves as well. She began searching for a subject of conversation that might distract Willow.

"There it is!" Willow cried suddenly. "I hear it!"

"What do you hear?"

Caroline strained to pick up anything at all over the noise of the sports car engine. Willow had rolled down the window on her side. Caroline thought Willow might have done that because the car heater was on, though set at a low temperature. Caroline had never been very well adapted to the climate up here, and tonight's chill was no exception.

"It has to be one of the men Justin hires to follow me," she said, more agitated than ever. "It just has to be."

Caroline rolled her own window down a few inches and listened again. "What are you talking about, Willow?" she asked after a few seconds. "I don't hear anything."

"You must hear it. A motorcycle. One of them drives a big black motorcycle. I can hear it. He must be pretty far behind us now, but he'll catch up. You must drive faster!"

What Caroline could hear was the growing frenzy in Willow's voice. "I don't hear any motorcycle," Caroline began.

"That's because you're not used to listening for it. I've had to learn to watch and listen every waking moment. That's how I spend my life now. Watching and listening."

There was a tremble of hysteria in Willow's words, and Caroline hurried to calm her down. "Willow, isn't there a possibility you could be exaggerating some of this just a little?" she asked in a steady, soothing tone.

Willow wasn't soothed. She grabbed Caroline's arm, nearly causing her to lose her grip on the wheel. "I am not exaggerating! Not in the least," Willow shrilled. "It is every bit as bad as I say it is. Sometimes worse. You have to believe me. You have to drive faster, or he'll catch up, and I dread to think what he might do to us if he's discovered my flight!"

Willow had both hands clamped on Caroline's arm, and Caroline could feel her throat tightening with anxiety. She had to get Willow under control and keep herself calm as well.

"All right, I'll drive faster," she said pressing down a bit on the accelerator.

"Faster! Faster than that!" Willow lunged toward her as if intending to get her foot on the gas pedal and push it to the floor herself.

"Calm down, Willow," Caroline said in a tone that was more firm than soothing now. "I'm driving as fast as I safely can on this road."

"Safe? How can you talk about being safe with the devil himself behind us?"

They had reached the turn to the Burrville Road. Caroline had to slow for the flashing caution light, and as she did the roar of the engine quieted some. In that instant she thought she might have heard the higher pitched sound of a motorcycle whining in the distance. Again, she strained to hear, hoping she was simply picking up on Willow's terror.

Willow had let go of Caroline's arm, but now she grabbed it again. "Go! Go!" she shrieked.

Caroline tromped down on the gas, and the small car cornered with a screech of tires. There might be someone after them; then again, there might not. Caroline couldn't be sure about that one way or the other right now, but what she could be sure of was that she had to get Willow out of this car as soon as possible, before her hysteria caused an accident.

"Okay. I'm driving faster," said Caroline. "Now you have to let go of my arm, stop shouting at me and let me drive."

After a brief hesitation, Willow did as she was told, cringing into her bucket seat and clasping her arms tightly around herself. Her breathing was heavy and rapid between the small, sobbing sounds she apparently could not control.

Willow's agitation was contagious. Besides, living alone for many years had taught Caroline to err on the side of caution where menace was concerned, and that went double for a dark night and a deserted country road. Willow didn't need to goad Caroline into pushing the little car to eat up the remaining few miles to the Burrville house in record time.

The windows of the house were dark, and Caroline was uneasy about leaving her friend there alone, but Willow insisted she take off instantly to reduce the risk of disclosing her temporary hideout. So Caroline backed out of the driveway and onto the narrow, high-crowned road that led to the highway once more. Willow was still standing in front of the darkened house, her arms clutched around her slender body, as Caroline drove away around the bend in the road and out of sight.

All the way back to the hotel, she pondered what had happened. Clearly Willow was terrified of her husband, but whether there were real grounds for her fears was still in question. Caroline had agreed to help her get out of Watertown, at least for a while. She might calm down some if she could be away from

Justin for a time and think things through more rationally. She could stay at Caroline's house in Westchester or with friends of hers in New York City. Then, when Willow was less emotional about the situation, Caroline intended to help her friend get to the bottom of what was really going on in her marriage. After all, what good was it to have connections with a therapy center if you couldn't take advantage of its services?

Caroline was reflecting on those many services when the unmistakable sound of a motorcycle roaring into the hotel parking lot made her gasp and instinctively check the car door to make sure it was locked.

She peered through the windshield into the shadows at the restaurant side of the motel where the bike had stopped but went on rumbling. She could make out the shape of rider and machine, big and black against the lighter colored brick of the wall behind them. The rider twisted the throttle to make the powerful engine beneath him explode to an intimidating pitch. Then he—or could it be she?—let the bike decelerate in a barrage of lesser eruptions to a still intimidating idle.

Caroline told herself there were hundreds of big black bikes in the north country. Powerful vehicles were a considerable part of the way of life up here. This was not necessarily the biker Willow had heard behind them earlier, if she had in fact heard anything at all.

Still, these reasonable assurances wore thinner for Caroline by the second. With each new rev of the cycle engine her heart thudded faster and higher in her throat until she could barely swallow, and when she did, her mouth was parched by fear.

She tried taking a deep breath to quiet herself, realizing that she couldn't spend the night cringing in the parking lot. The biker hadn't come anywhere near her. Surely she would be safe if she simply got out of the car and walked quickly but calmly into the hotel.

She pushed the door open and scrambled out much more rapidly than she usually managed from the low-slung roadster. She closed the door behind her and was about to lock it when the biker throttled the engine again and kept up the reverberating roar.

Caroline forgot her resolve to remain calm and began to run.

Why had she parked so far from the door? She thanked God for giving her the sense to wear low-heeled shoes on all but a very few occasions in her life, including this one. She also thanked God that she had always been a strong runner.

As she neared the hotel, she was gulping air, probably more from adrenaline than exhaustion. She had headed for the secondary entrance closest at hand, which happened to lead onto her wing. She realized that the bike had gone suddenly silent. The driver could very possibly be running after her!

Just then another terrifying thought pumped through her. She gulped so hard she almost gagged. What if she needed her room key to open this side door? She tried to remember exactly where she had put the card key amidst the clutter in her bag. She would never be able to find it in time.

Please, let the door be open, she prayed as she reached for the press bar.

An instant later her prayers were answered, but she waited till she was safely inside her room before mumbling her thanks heavenward. Her heart continued to pound.

MICHAEL SCHAEFFER sat back in his maple-finished captain's chair and feigned just enough interest in the dinner table conversation to know vaguely what was going on. They were the only party left in the hotel dining room, but, as usual, the table was full for Justin Fowler's monthly dinners.

As was also usual by this point in the evening, after a few highballs or beers, the "boys" were getting boisterous, laughing too loudly and talking over one another in a contest to be heard. Justin could have quieted them down with a word, but Mike understood why he did not.

The boozy camaraderie among his self-appointed chamber of commerce. He'd told Mike that a spirit of brotherhood was essential to keeping the guys off their duffs, where they'd all been languishing before Justin came to town a few years ago and began kicking those duffs into gear.

The "Young Turks" he called them, a handpicked collection of local businessmen and officials he claimed were young enough not to have ossified into the rigid patterns of some of their elders. They still had enough "juice," as Justin put it, to spearhead some necessary changes in this town that had seen far better days.

Sometimes Mike wondered why he had been included in this group. He certainly was not as gung ho as Justin would have liked him to be, and he didn't cotton to Justin's "guidance" the way so many others did. In fact, if Justin had his way, Mike would be running for mayor in the next election.

"Don't you want to prove you can win?" Justin had asked many times.

"Why would I want to do that?" Mike always answered.

Justin would shake his head in disbelief and then launch into a defense of his plans for Mike, claiming the town needed Mike's leadership. The man never gave up. Mike had to admire him for that. But Mike didn't need to be a leader. He had gotten all of that out of his system in the jungle twenty-odd years ago.

He had been full of pith and vinegar when he'd first enlisted, eighteen years old and set on showing the world what he was made of. He guessed he had done that. He had done his duty with valor, as they say, even stuck his neck out too far for his own good in more than one fire fight when a fellow needed a hand. There had been medals to make it official. They'd even called him a hero.

But those days, when he would go out looking for a challenge just to see if he could beat it, were behind him now. He had proven whatever it was he had to prove to himself and everybody else, and, thank God, he had gotten out alive and in one piece. That was enough of a major personal victory to last him most likely his whole life. All he wanted now was to do the job that the Nam had set him up for in a lot of ways— and to live his life simply and as he saw fit.

At least that was all he had wanted until two or three hours ago. Then he'd seen Caro Hardin again. Now he was beginning to wonder if there might not be one thing left he had to prove.

He could still smell the scent of her, something subtle and expensive that you probably couldn't buy around here. The memory of it had stayed with him, the same way the memory of Caro herself had stayed with him, all these years. How many times had she popped into his thoughts since he had last seen her before tonight? Maybe a million? That was probably a big exaggeration, but it didn't feel like one to him.

Even when he had been with Barbara, even before they finally admitted to each other that they should have stayed friends and not tried to be husband and wife, even then Caro had been in a corner of his heart, a symbol of something forever lost to him, forever inaccessible. He had watched her grow up and felt an unusual pang of loss when she left town.

That kiss of theirs all those years ago had been pure and innocent as could be, possibly more so than any other kiss he had ever experienced. Maybe that was why it had stuck in his memory. Maybe he had held on to it as a reminder that such purity and innocence existed, if only to be forever out of his reach.

He had never really believed he would see her again. And until this very second he had never considered the possibility, no matter how slight, that she might *not* be forever out of his reach. Perhaps he could reclaim a piece of his former innocence.

She would probably tell him to take a hike, but he had to see her again or never stop wondering. He pushed away from the table and waved off Justin's protest against his leaving so soon.

"You would be proud of me, Justin," Mike might have said aloud but didn't. "There is something worth sticking my neck out for after all."

Chapter Three

Mike had faced danger in his job. Maybe not as much as if he did that job in Manhattan or Chicago or L.A. Still, there had been some pretty scary times over the years, but never anything as unsettling as what he was facing now.

He stared at the closed door of Caroline's hotel room. He had gone through doors heavier than this in one charge. But this particular drama didn't pump up his boldness and make him strong. It left him feeling weak and way too vulnerable. He had messed up somewhere along the way, and because of that maybe nothing could ever go right again. He hadn't done all of his paperwork with attention to detail up front, the way a good cop was supposed to do.

He couldn't remember having such a strong urge to run away since Nam, when he was under fire. He was under fire now, too, and just like over there, he had no idea what was going to happen next and even less of a sense of control over whatever it turned out to be. But as it had been back then, there was no choice but to do what he had come for.

He raised his fist, hesitated a moment, then knocked, stunned that he was fairly cowering at the door of a woman he could probably pick up with one hand.

No response. Maybe she wasn't here. That was most unlikely, however. He had checked the parking lot for her car after learning the make and model from her hotel registration card. You could get away with things like that in a small town where you knew everybody, including the night desk clerk.

Would she be annoyed to see him at her door? In the old days she'd had a tough, defensive way about her now and then, as if always expecting somebody to put her down or treat her badly. Was she still like that? Was she anything at all the way she used to be?

There was only one way to find out. He knocked again, a bit more resolutely this time. Out of habit he had stood out of range of the peephole.

"Who is it?" Caroline said from beyond the door. She did not sound pleased, but she didn't sound angry, either. She sounded . . . something else. What was it?

"Caro, it's Mike Schaeffer." He stepped in front of the eyepiece so she could be certain.

"What do you want?"

He hadn't expected her to fall into his arms, but he hadn't thought she would bite his head off, either. He also wasn't really sure what he did want here, so he hesitated before answering. In those few seconds, the door inched open on its chain, and he could see one of Caroline's huge brown eyes looking out at him. He didn't find any welcome there. She had been coolly polite in the lobby earlier. Now she seemed closer to hostile. And Mike knew he had made a big mistake by coming here.

"I wasn't expecting visitors," she said with frostiness in her voice.

"You're right. It's late. I shouldn't have disturbed you. I just wanted to say hello." Mike forced himself to stop short of asking what was wrong. Doubtless *he* was what was wrong.

"That was very nice of you," Caroline said without sounding any less frosty. "But I have to go now."

"Sure. I understand. Good night."

"Good night."

She hadn't taken the chain off the door as they talked. Consequently, hardly more than a second was required for her to shut the door with a firm thud, followed by a turn of the lock.

He sensed that Caroline was still on the other side of the door, peering at him. Could she see in his eyes that now he did want to break the door down, muscle it out of the frame, chain and all, stride over it like a marauder over a drawbridge into her castle, sweep her into his arms and steal her away?

As he contemplated his own wayward reaction, it suddenly dawned on him what he had heard in her voice and seen in her eyes. He remembered that look. It had been in her eyes, along with her seemingly peevish defensiveness when she was a girl. Other than her obvious annoyance, he was sure he had seen fear. If he hadn't been so antsy about meeting her again, he would have recognized it right off.

Of course, there was nothing so out of line about her being a little spooked. She was all alone in town, and there had been a knock on her door well after dark. She had looked out, and nobody was there. That could spook anybody.

But Mike sensed that wasn't why she had sent him away even after she found out who he was. She hadn't been in her night clothes, either. He could see through the door opening that she was still fully dressed including her jacket, as if she might have just gotten in. It would have been no trouble for her to come out with him to the bar for a drink. He now realized that was probably what he had been hoping for when he showed up here, that they would go somewhere and talk for a while.

Caroline had made it very clear that she was not interested in having a drink with him or talking with him or doing anything with him. All she wanted was for him to stop making a pest of himself and leave her alone. Now Mike had no choice but to do just that. Before turning to walk away, he managed a brief smile at the peephole. He hoped that smile would make something else very clear—that he had absolutely no intention of ever bothering her this way, or any other way, either, ever again.

CAROLINE DIDN'T fall asleep until dawn, and then she suffered chaotic, intense and unsettling dreams. Worse, she didn't so much wake up as feel jolted into consciousness, shaking inside and clutched by a cold, white terror.

She had the impression that something had scared her awake and could still be here in this room. The hotel blackout curtains made it dark as night.

She reached out and fumbled for the button at the base of the bedside lamp. The movement required an act of will; what she really wanted to do was dive headfirst under the covers.

The light snapped on to reveal nothing more remarkable than the remnants of last night's junk-food binge littering the nightstand. She had waited nearly an hour after Mike Schaeffer left before creeping out of her room and down the hall to the anteroom that held the vending machines. She might know some psychology but she was still a human being. When she was under stress, sometimes nothing was more comforting than a combination of too much sugar and too much salt, and she had been heartened to discover that this hotel's vending area was a treasure trove of both.

Getting back to her room from there had not been so pleasant. That was when she'd experienced the near panic that had carried over into her dreams and later jolted her awake. She had felt that somebody or something was after her. Her sense of that had been too powerful to shake off or reason herself out of. She had hurried back to her room, locked the door and chained it.

Her next step, now, was to analyze the causes. Okay, one: the biker had scared her. Then, not long after she made her mad dash from the parking lot to her room, there had been a knock on her door. She hadn't been expecting anyone. Nobody even knew she was here. Who could it be? She couldn't see anything through the security lens in the door. Was somebody hiding out there? Should she call the desk clerk for help?

She had called out to see who it was and been shocked to hear Mike Schaeffer's voice respond. What was he doing there? How had he found her room? Hotels never gave out information on guests, especially women. So had he silently stalked her, followed her here? How else could he have known which room she was in? This was a big hotel.

That thought brought a renewed hint of panic—along with a mental image of Mike as the man on the motorcycle, tracking her and Willow to Burrville, then tailing Caroline back here all the way to her room.

He could be one of the cronies of Justin's Willow had talked about. He could be anybody or anything. She had not seen or heard of him in too many years to know anything for certain. All she did know was that he was no longer the sensitive wounded young warrior of her adolescent fantasies. He was a man big enough and strong enough to hurt her if he had a mind to.

Of course, she had not let him in, and he had gone away. After that she had lain awake for a long time. Even the junk food hadn't soothed her much. The realization that she had absolutely no idea what she might have walked into up here had hit her with a sickening thud. The people she had known all those years ago would be much changed now. But what had they changed into?

She was little more than a stranger here in the north country. She had no close connections anymore. Her father was dead. Her mother had moved away. Caroline had not maintained contact with anybody but Willow, and even that had been sporadic. Thus, this was uncharted territory for her now. The likes of Mike Schaeffer might appear friendly on the surface, but were they friendly underneath? She had no way of knowing, and caution was in order.

Panic, however, was not. Panic, whether brought on by a dream or a real-life incident, only hindered the ability to act in one's own defense.

Still, the tremors persisted for the better part of an hour after her rude awakening. Even when she finally did venture out of her hotel room, dread clung to her like the rank, stagnant scent of a place that has been closed up too long.

She vowed to drive out the feeling with a hearty breakfast in the hotel dining room, but a cup of coffee and a roll were all she could manage to get down. Then she headed out to meet Willow.

The house in Burrville turned out to be quite attractive in the daylight, a two-story clapboard bungalow painted white with dark red roof shingles. There was a small porch on the driveway side, hung with a few flower pots that could have used some attention, but the lawn was neatly mowed. There were no cars in sight, though an old barn down the slope behind the house could be the garage.

Caroline rang the doorbell and heard two notes resonate inside. She waited a few moments. When there was no response, she rang again. She couldn't see in, the blinds were closed. There was no answer to her second ring, so she knocked loudly. Even as the echo of her knuckles on the wood faded away, she knew there was nobody here. The stillness of the place was too complete.

She called out all the same. "Willow, are you here? Willow, it's me, Caroline." More stillness was the reply.

Caroline rattled the door handle, but it was locked. Where was Willow? Their plans had been very definite to meet here and make arrangements for Willow to get away for a while. Caroline checked her watch. She was right on time.

Could Willow have been confused about their plan? Could she have decided to leave town on her own without waiting for Caroline? That was highly unlikely, given how desperate she had been for Caroline to come up here in the first place. Had something happened to her?

Caroline had to get into this house. She tried the two windows on either side of the door, but they were both locked. She left the stoop and walked around to the back of the house. That was when she saw the open window. It was raised only a few inches, as if to let in some air.

Caroline's rational processes clicked into place. It was unusual for north country people, especially those out here in the countryside, to leave a window open without a screen in the summertime when the insect population was at its peak.

The window itself, at closer glance, made her even more suspicious. There were definite tool marks on the sill and lower section of the frame. Someone had jimmied his way in here. Caroline was certain of that. She hesitated only a moment before pushing the window open wide enough to fit through and climb in. Niceties like trespassing were less important than finding out what had happened to Willow.

Right away Caroline could tell this was a man's house. There were signs of that everywhere—the pockets of clutter and dust that most women wouldn't be able to live with, the stack of *Sports Illustrated* magazines on the kitchen counter, the odd pieces of male clothing and paraphernalia here and there. Caroline could not help but wonder what Willow had been doing staying in a man's house. Could there be some foundation to Justin's accusations that she was unfaithful?

Whatever the circumstances behind Willow's coming here last night, she definitely was not here now. In fact, there was no sign that she had ever been here.

Caroline felt a suggestion of her former fear once more. Then she reminded herself that maybe Willow had changed her mind overnight and had gone back home to work things out with Justin.

That possibility brought with it a sigh of relief. Caroline hurried to the phone she had noticed on the kitchen wall and dialed Willow's number. It was foolish to jump to conclusions, especially sinister ones, before exploring more hopeful alternatives.

An older woman answered and, at Caroline's question, identified herself as the housekeeper. At first she would only say that Mrs. Fowler wasn't in. It took several minutes of Caroline's best persuasive tactics to get the woman to expand on that. Finally she said exactly what Caroline didn't want to hear. Willow had left some time early last evening and had taken a suitcase with her. She had not been home since.

Caroline hung up the phone and considered what to do next. Her first instinct was to call Justin. Then she remembered something Willow had said last night.

"If anything happens to me, I implore you not to listen to Justin's explanation of what it was. He will charm you to death with his lies, the same way he charms everyone."

At the time, Caroline had chalked that up to melodrama brought on by her friend's overwrought state.
Now she wasn't so sure. One of the things a counselor
learns very early on is to heed the testimony of the patient. Whether the words themselves are factually true
or not doesn't matter as much as the emotional truth
beneath those words. Unless one was dealing with abnormal psychology, that emotional reaction was sure
to indicate something of consequence.

Caroline felt very strongly that she must apply that
principle to Willow. She would not call Justin. She
would go to the police instead.

THE POLICE STATION was located exactly where it had
been for as far back as Caroline could remember, in
the municipal building diagonally across the street
corner from her hotel. She parked in the lot near her
room and walked over, crossing to the front of the office of the local newspaper, then again to the opposite
side of the street. Along the way, she kept seeing people who looked vaguely familiar to her. She couldn't
put names to any of the faces. She suspected she might
be imagining the recognition out of a need to make
some contact with her own history here. She wondered how strong that need might be.

She had asked at the desk for the detective in
charge, and the sergeant on duty had brought her to
this office to wait. There was no nameplate on the desk
or the door. The only personal touches were some citations on the wall. Caroline walked over to look at
them. She couldn't seem to stop hoping that she would
run into someone she knew from the past, instead of

only strangers that made her feel as if this might be somebody else's hometown but not hers.

When she saw the name on the citations, she could hardly believe her eyes. She wasn't sure what to think, except that she needed to get out of here.

"May I help you?"

Caroline turned to face Mike Schaeffer. And she fleetingly registered that he looked at least as uneasy as she.

"You didn't tell me you were an officer of the law," she said, trying to sound casual.

"We didn't have much of an opportunity to get reacquainted."

Caroline felt herself beginning to blush at the subtle reminder of her refusal to talk to him last night.

"Do you drive a motorcycle?" she asked abruptly.

He looked surprised. Had she caught him in a guilty secret—that he had been the one following her or he was simply puzzled by the out-of-left-field question?

"I ride a bike sometimes," he said. "But not in the line of duty."

"I see that you've been cited more than a few times for the way you perform that duty," Caroline said. She nodded toward the wall of plaques. "You must be quite the hero."

"Not really. Is that what you came here to talk about? My citations?"

Caroline stared at him, then said, "No, I'm here to report a missing person."

"You've been in town less than twenty-four hours and you're already missing somebody?"

Mike crossed to the desk and indicated the chair facing it. She sat down, watching him as he opened first one drawer, then another, shuffling through the papers there till he found what was apparently the appropriate form. Then he opened yet another drawer and rummaged around till he produced a pen.

The delay gave Caroline a few moments to observe him. He was out of uniform, of course, being a detective. There was a carelessness about his manner of dressing that was endearing in a way, and he could have used a haircut. His shirt tugged a bit across his broad shoulders. He must have been working out, building muscle, because there was definitely no fat on him anywhere she could see.

She couldn't help thinking that if she were his wife, she would make certain he changed his shirt size to accommodate that added broadness. That thought clicked with an earlier one, about there being no family pictures in this office. She would bet just about anything that Mike was the type to keep a photograph of his wife on his desk—if he had a wife any longer.

"Name?" he asked.

"What?" she stammered.

"I'll need details of the disappearance," he pointed out.

"Oh, yes. Of course."

He watched her and waited. His arm rested easily on the desk blotter, pen poised. If he was feeling any concern, either about the nature of the case or her presence here this morning, he didn't let it show.

"A close friend of mine is missing," she said. "We agreed last night that we would meet this morning, but she didn't show up." Caroline realized how absurd that sounded and hastened to clarify why she was making this report. "Her husband had been menacing her, making threats. I was arranging for her to get away from here for a while. I think our meeting this morning was too important to her for her to have missed out on it voluntarily. That's why I am here."

"What is your friend's name?"

"Willow Gilchrist Fowler. Her husband is Justin Fowler."

Mike put his pen down. "Yes, I know them," he said. "And I doubt that anything has happened to your friend that she didn't want to have happen."

"What do you mean by that?"

"I mean that I'm acquainted with this couple, and I doubt that Justin Fowler is—" he waved a hand "—'menacing his wife and making threats.' I would agree that there are problems between those two, but I really don't think they're the ones you describe."

"What makes you so sure of that?" Caroline was beginning to feel condescended to, and she didn't like it one bit.

"All I can say is that I know something of both parties, and in my opinion you have the wrong fix on the situation." He picked up the form he had been writing on and folded it down the middle, obviously preparing to discard it.

"Are you refusing to take my report?"

"I'm not refusing you anything. I simply think you're operating on incorrect information here."

"I came here to file an official complaint, and if you don't intend to take that complaint seriously, you'll have to give me something more than vague generalities."

Mike hesitated a long moment before speaking. "I suppose this comes under the heading of common knowledge, so I wouldn't be violating any confidences by telling you."

"Then tell away," Caroline snapped.

"First of all, Justin Fowler is a man of some importance and prestige in this town. And he's made no secret of the fact that he's the one having problems in that marriage. Knowing his wife's history, I have to say that his accusations aren't hard to believe."

"What accusations?"

Mike sighed as if he definitely was not enjoying this. "Justin claims that Willow has been unfaithful to him."

"She told me about those claims of his." This conversation was beginning to make Caroline angry. "Willow says her husband's accusations are false, and I believe her."

Mike sighed again. "You must have known what a flirt she was before they got married . . . and there's been talk about her since."

"Every woman who isn't a total hausfrau gets talked about in this town. As for her 'flirting,' Willow is simply a gregarious, vivacious person. That kind of behavior in a woman is often misinterpreted by men of a primitive mind-set." Caroline was growing more upset by the minute, and for more reasons than her friend's alleged flirting.

"I get the distinct feeling you include me in that category," Mike said. "And since you have included me, I will tell you that I happen to be one of the men Mrs. Fowler has flirted with. Believe me, there's no room for misinterpretation."

That statement knocked the wind out of Caroline's sails for a moment. She took that moment to recover and was about to ask whether that flirting had happened before or after Willow married Justin when Mike's phone rang. He answered it, and almost instantly his entire manner changed. The tensing of his facial muscles was subtle, but Caroline saw it. He responded in clipped monosyllables, scribbling notes on a small pad he had pulled from his pocket. He put the phone down and was out of his chair in one taut movement.

"I'm sorry to cut this off so abruptly," he said, "but something has come up." He pulled a light-weight jacket off the back of the chair.

"Are you going to check on Willow's whereabouts?" Caroline had risen from her chair, as well.

"Twenty-four hours must elapse before an official missing-persons can be filed. I'll let you know if I hear anything before that. You'll be staying on across the street, I assume."

He was standing over her now.

"I'll be in town a while longer. At least, I think I will."

She was trying not to sound flustered by his closeness, but she wasn't sure how well she was succeeding. Nor had she managed to disguise her irritation at being shunted aside. And by Mike Schaeffer, of all people. On top of that, Caroline had planned a brief visit to Watertown, maybe just enough time to give Willow the support she needed. After that, she had hoped to slip out of town before being here in the north country could get under her skin the way it had so often in the past. Now she was afraid she might be stuck here for a while, and Mike Schaeffer was definitely getting under her skin.

He put his hands on her shoulders and moved her gently out of his path. "I'll make a point of talking to you before you leave," he said.

Then he was out the door in two long strides and across the outer office in a few more, signaling another plainclothes officer to follow.

As Caroline emerged from the office in his wake, she overheard a policeman questioning the desk sergeant. "What's all that about?" he asked, pointing after Mike.

"They found a body down by the river," the sergeant answered. "Looks like a suspicious death to the patrol that reported it."

So that was why Mike took off in such a hurry, thought Caroline. She could imagine where finding Willow would fall on his list of priorities now.

Despite what he had said about Willow and Justin Fowler, Caroline still believed the situation deserved looking into. If Mike wasn't willing to be the detective in the case, maybe she would have to take matters into her own hands. At least until she had something to make Mike sit up and take notice.

Caroline was on her way out of the police station, doing her best to squelch the familiarity of that thought, when another thought struck her, so chilling it made the unseasonably cold day feel warm by comparison.

What if the body they had found was Willow's? What if she wasn't exaggerating her claims about Justin, as Mike obviously believed? What if there really had been someone chasing them last night? What if that person had shown up at the Burrville house after Caroline left? What if...

Caroline began to run toward the parking lot behind the municipal building. A car was tearing out of the opposite end of the lot and pulling into the street. Caroline waved her arms frantically and called Mike's name, but he kept on driving. She stamped her foot in frustration.

"Something wrong, lady?"

A uniformed patrolman had obviously taken notice of her antics and was looking her over now in that suspicious way police have.

Caroline opened her mouth to babble out her fears that her best friend might be lying on a riverbank, but the skeptical look on the officer's face stopped her cold. No way would she invite someone to label her a hysterical female.

"There's nothing wrong, Officer," she said. "Nothing at all."

She felt him watching her as she walked back toward the front of the building, and she did her best to believe that what she had told the officer was true.

Chapter Four

Mike had heard it said that the daily life of a soldier or a cop hardened a person until he didn't feel much of anything one way or another anymore. Mike knew that wasn't true, at least not for him. The more times he witnessed the end of life, especially when that end had been violent, the more it got to him, grating along his nerve endings like a fingernail on a blackboard. At such times, he kept himself hard on the outside so the screeching of those nerves wouldn't escape and freak out everybody around him.

Fortunately, this one had not been a messy death. To the nonprofessional, it would have looked like the old guy got stumbling drunk, fell down and hit his head on a rock. End of story, for him and for the case. Mike and his men, on the other hand, were professionals. Joe Palumbo, Mike's detective junior grade, had already noted the inconsistencies with that accidental-fall scenario.

Palumbo was shorter than Mike and appeared softer as well because of a tendency toward fleshiness and a developing paunch. But Mike knew better. Under Palumbo's extra flesh was a strong, wiry guy who could come on tough and deliver on that threat. Palumbo had done his own time in Nam, and though they never talked about it, that particular piece of common history had created a bond between the men. They would watch each other's backs forever if necessary, whether in the jungle or out here on the streets.

"There's a lot of dried blood around the scalp wound," Palumbo said, "but no stain underneath the body or on the rock he's supposed to have hit."

He pointed to the slab of granite sticking out of the riverbank. There were numerous embedded rocks and boulders along Black River shore, and a good many of them had sharp edges like this one. It was no place to go stumbling around in the dark, particularly if you had just finished off a pint of Jim Beam, as the empty bottle in the brown bag near the body seemed to indicate.

"Expensive liquor for a transient," Mike remarked. He had never seen this guy before, and he would have if he were a local. "Did he have anything else interesting on him?" The pockets of the dead man's stained trench coat and frayed pants had already been turned out.

"Very interesting, as a matter of fact. He didn't have anything on him."

"Nothing at all?"

"I thought that would get your attention." Palumbo had often said how much he got a kick out of surprising Mike, then watching the wheels click into motion.

"Would you say somebody cleaned him out?" Mike had knelt down next to the still form on the ground but didn't disturb anything.

"Looks that way to me."

"So it could be robbery."

"Could be, but I can't imagine why anybody would think this old guy had anything worth rolling him for."

Mike nodded. The deceased did look too decrepit to be worth much. "Then again, he was drinking the good stuff, so maybe he'd come into a stake and let the wrong person know about it."

"Possibly. But why would they take absolutely everything the old guy was carrying? He must have had a pocket comb or some tissues or at least some lint on him besides cash."

"I'm not sure about a comb," Mike said, noting the dead man's straggly hair. "But you've got a point. Why do you think they would have cleaned him out like this?" he asked, though he already knew what Palumbo would answer.

This kind of verbal brain-picking was no game. By bouncing every detail, no matter how obvious, off each other, he and Palumbo often came up with something that belied the obvious. That was part of the art of being a detective. Many crimes involve secrets, plus somebody intent upon covering up those secrets. In this case perhaps by disguising what really happened to make it look like something else.

"They could have been trying to make it hard for us to find out who this guy is," said Palumbo, echoing Mike's suspicions.

"Did they leave the labels in his clothes?"

"Yeah, but what he's wearing looks like thrift shop stuff or something out of a Salvation Army bin. Nothing you could ever trace. So what would be the point of bothering with the labels?"

Mike straightened up and began pacing off the distance from the body to the road. "I don't see any signs of a body being dragged here."

"That would be easy enough to hide in this kind of scrub grass."

Mike nodded. He was nearly convinced that Palumbo was right in his assessment of the scene, but cops tend to be suspicious by nature and see possible evil doings underlying just about everything. Mike's job was to guard against that. He had to think like the defense lawyer who would be chopping the prosecution's case to smithereens if it ever got to court. Giving Palumbo the third degree was a useful start.

"Who called it in?" Mike asked.

"That's another interesting point," said Palumbo, sounding deceptively casual and thereby alerting Mike to another ringer of a surprise. "It was one of your buddies from the Saturday Night Winners' Circle."

That was Palumbo's sarcastic name for Justin Fowler's young community leaders group. Mike wasn't sure whether Palumbo reacted that way because he hadn't been included in those get-togethers like the one last night or because of something less personal that bothered him about the group.

"I'd say this part of town was way off the beaten path for an upscale dude like him, especially on a Sunday morning. Wouldn't you agree?"

Palumbo cocked his head in the direction of the police cars and the gaggle of rubberneckers they were attracting. Palumbo was right on target this time. Tim Manders was a long way from his neighborhood. The town's more respectable citizenry seldom ventured past the old railroad tracks to this low road by the river.

Manders was in the real estate business. He had taken over his father's successful firm several years ago and, according to local gossip, had managed to drive it at least partway into the ground and was working on completing the job. Still, Mike doubted he was down-and-out enough to be handling properties in this neck of the woods, especially since Justin Fowler claimed to be working with Tim on some new financial strategies that would have Manders Realty headed toward high times again soon.

And there was another even more compelling reason Tim Manders's presence here was something of a mystery. First of all, it was Sunday morning, as Palumbo had mentioned. Second, it was summertime. Third...well, that was what Mike intended to find out about right now.

"Hey, Tim. How ya doin'?" Mike said, extending his hand with a jovial smile. "We missed you when you had to leave the dinner early last night. You know how Justin likes to have the full team together whenever he can manage it."

"I had business to attend to. It couldn't be helped," Tim said. He was nervous, and it showed. There were beads of perspiration on his pink forehead, even though it wasn't a very warm day.

"Well, business always comes first. Nobody would agree with that more than Justin."

"Ain't that the truth," Palumbo said.

Mike let the remark pass. Palumbo wasn't fond of Justin, but this wasn't the place for airing personal prejudices. Besides, Mike had something else on his mind.

"You know, Tim, I could have sworn you said you had to leave last night to go down to your summer place because your wife was expecting you. Could I have been mistaken about that?"

The rather rotund man turned pinker and damper than ever. "That's right. I had to get down there, so I couldn't stay as late with you guys as I usually do."

"I thought you just said you were tied up with business," Palumbo said.

"I—I completed the business first."

"If you did your business, then drove all the way to your summer place afterward, what would have brought you back to town so early on a Sunday morning?" Palumbo asked with his usual talent for the bad-cop role.

Tim looked to Mike as if their acquaintance might cut him some slack here, but Mike only smiled and waited for his answer.

"It was cold," Tim said, obviously relieved to have come up with that response. "It was so cold at the river that my wife decided to bring the kids home."

"When did you find that out?" Mike asked. "Last night or this morning?"

Tim frowned. "I found it out last night," he said in a petulant tone. "After my business appointment I called my wife, and she told me she and the kids were coming back to town this morning."

"So you never went to the summer place after all. Is that right?" Mike asked.

Tim stared at him for a moment, as if trying to find some trap in the question. "That's right. I didn't see any reason to run down there when the family was coming straight back here this morning."

"And what brings you to this part of town on a Sunday morning?" Palumbo asked. "It's not exactly on your way to church."

"Business. I had some business on the north side, and I took a shortcut through here."

"You sure do a lot of business, don't you?" Palumbo remarked.

"Yes, I do. Is there anything wrong with that?"

"Not a thing," said Mike before Tim became even more defensive. "And we want to thank you for calling this in. We appreciate it."

"If I'd known it was going to tie up my whole morning, I might not have," Tim said belligerently.

"We won't keep you much longer," Mike said. "I just need you to tell me exactly what happened here and what you saw."

"I don't have the slightest idea what happened, and all I saw was that guy lying by the road. I thought maybe he was hurt, so I stopped to help. I didn't know he'd turn out to be dead."

"I bet he didn't know that either till it was too late," Palumbo quipped.

Mike gave him a quelling look.

"Have you ever seen this man before?" Mike asked.

"Him?" Tim sounded offended by the very suggestion. "Of course not."

"Then you have no previous relationship with the victim?" Palumbo pressed the point.

"Victim of what? I thought he fell and hit his head."

"That's just a police term, Tim," Mike said. "By the way, you said you were taking a shortcut this morning. A shortcut from where to where?"

Manders was really red in the face now. "From over there to over here." He gestured angrily first down the road and then up it. "Look here, Mike. I did my duty as a public-minded citizen, and now I find myself being interrogated. I don't think this is right, and—and..." He seemed to be searching for what more to say. "And if you ask me one more thing, I'm going to have to call my lawyer."

"That won't be necessary, Tim. Sorry we held you up so long. You can go now. I'll be in touch if there are any further details we need to go over," Mike said. "We appreciate your cooperation."

Mike shook Tim's hand and watched him stalk off in a huff to his dark blue BMW.

"Yup," Palumbo said, watching the expensive sedan cruise away. "Doing your duty as a public-minded citizen can sure ruin your day. I bet we made him late for Sunday brunch."

"You can ease up on the good-cop bad-cop routine now, Palumbo. It's just the two of us here."

"You know you love it when I do that," Palumbo grinned. "Just as long as I don't let on that you're really the bad cop underneath."

Mike didn't even flinch. "Let's get a full workup on this case, no matter who might put up a squawk about the money it would cost."

"Are you thinking what I'm thinking?" Palumbo asked.

"I was thinking that this road isn't a shortcut from anywhere to anywhere."

"Yeah. I know."

THE HOUSE on St. Mary Street was exactly as Caroline remembered it, right down to the wicker porch furniture with the green-striped cushions where she and Willow had spent hours beyond number carrying on about the things adolescent girls carry on about—boys mostly, as Caroline recalled. She was so caught up in her nostalgia that she almost forgot how frightened she was that the body on the riverbank could be her friend. For the moment at least, the past felt more real than the rest. Della Gilchrist even came to the door in what looked like the same apron she had worn all those years ago.

"Mercy me, it's Caro Hardin!" she cried. The delight in her eyes could hardly have been more genuine. Mrs. Gilchrist swung open the screen door and threw her arms around Caroline, though she had to stand on tiptoe to do so.

The tears had wet Caroline's cheeks before she knew they were in her eyes. She swallowed hard. If home was the place where someone truly cared about you, then she had come home at last. She returned the hug with equal warmth and held on extra tight for a moment, hoping to calm her fears about Willow's well-being.

"Della, I can't tell you how good it is to see you."

"Oh, yes, you can," said Della with a dimply smile that sparkled in her eyes. "And I'll be happy to listen, because I'm just as happy to see you. Come on inside. It's too chilly today to be out here on this porch."

Caroline followed Della inside, where the scent of the small house assailed her with memories. Every place has its own smell, and this place smelled to her like happiness. That was what she had found here when she was a teenager—a safe and happy haven from the tensions at home. She knew, even before Della led her through the dining room, that they would talk in the kitchen, just as they had in the old days.

Caroline sat down in the same chair she had taken back then, feeling for an instant as if she and Willow had just rushed in after school. Della would ask what had happened that day, and Willow would have a half-dozen anecdotes to tell, each tumbling over the other in her eagerness to share them with her mother and her best friend. Caroline might have come in thinking that nothing much worth talking about had gone on that day, but then she would catch the bug of Willow's enthusiasm, and soon she would be babbling along with her friend while Della listened and smiled and gave them good things to eat.

"I have some cookies," Della was saying now. "One of your favorites."

Caroline watched fondly as Della lifted the ceramic ears of the bear-shaped cookie jar and filled a flower-patterned plate with molasses drop cookies.

"I imagine you drink coffee these days instead of milk."

"Anything you serve would taste wonderful to me, Della."

Being in Watertown was rekindling so many old emotions, Caroline was beginning to wonder if she would explode from their power. This place—and Della—held so much sweetness for Caroline. Then, on the other, less positive side was the equally powerful rush of frustration that had always accompanied the kind of conversation she had with Mike. Right now, however, something more pressing than any of that was on her mind—the real reason she had come to St. Mary Street this afternoon.

"Della, do you know where Willow is?"

"I would guess that she's home this time on a Sunday, or maybe at their summer cottage. No, she wouldn't likely be there today. It's too cold out. Willow hates chilly weather. As I recall, you never cared much for it, either," Della nattered cheerfully.

"Their summer cottage? Where is that?" Caroline tried not to sound too anxious. She didn't want to alarm Della.

"Campbell's Point, right on the lake. Willow loves it there, but only when it's warm and sunny, not like today. Why are you asking? Isn't she at home?"

"No, she isn't."

"Well, she and Justin could be out for the day. I hope you can stay in town until they get back. She'd be heartbroken if she missed you!"

"Actually, I saw her last night. I was supposed to meet her again this morning, but she didn't show up. I was hoping you might know where I could find her."

"You say she isn't at home?"

Caroline hesitated a moment before answering. "The housekeeper says she hasn't been there all night and that she took a suitcase with her when she left."

Thankfully she didn't ask what had brought Caroline to town in the first place. Caroline hated to worry Della, but this situation could be serious. She prepared herself to assure her friend's mother that probably everything was all right and there'd just been a simple misunderstanding.

Instead, Della set the plate of cookies and a mug of steaming coffee in front of Caroline, then sat down across from her. "I don't think you need to worry, dear, not about Willow anyway. Every now and then she has to take what she calls a mini-vacation from life."

"What—what does she mean by that?" Caroline had taken a molasses cookie from the plate but couldn't bring herself to bite into it.

"You know how Willow is, so full of energy and all. Sometimes she gets a bit restless. When that happens she's likely to up and run off for a few days without so much as a by-your-leave to anybody. She's done that any number of times."

"Where does she go?"

"She has friends she visits mostly."

Caroline was beginning to feel somewhat relieved, even though she couldn't help wondering if some of those friends Willow visited might be male.

"She has visited you a few times over the years as I recall," Della went on.

Caroline suddenly felt ashamed for thinking uncharitable thoughts about her friend. "What does she get so restless with that she has to take off like that?" she asked.

"You of all people know the answer to that," Della said with a laugh. "You were so restless here yourself, you had to leave town altogether. Willow didn't make that choice. She wanted to stay, but every once in a while a bit of that same wandering fever overtakes her, and she disappears for a few days. Then she comes back again, good as new.''

''What does Justin think about all that?'' Caroline asked as she took another sip of the best coffee she'd had in years.

''He seems to understand, far as I can tell. But then, he's totally devoted to Willow, you know. I doubt there's a single thing in this world he wouldn't do for her. My Willow is so lucky to have found a husband like him. I thank the Lord for it.''

Caroline was puzzled. Della and Willow had always been close; Caroline had often envied the way Willow could tell her mother everything. Yet clearly Willow had not told Della what was going on with Justin. If so, Caroline should probably not divulge the confidence.

''I hope I haven't done something terribly out of line,'' Caroline began, ''but I was very concerned about Willow at the time, and it seemed the best thing to do.''

Della patted Caroline's hand. ''I doubt you have it in you to do anything too terrible, my dear. What is it?''

''I...I went to the police and told them Willow was missing.'' Caroline deliberately omitted what she had also told them about Justin.

''And what did the police have to say about that?''

''They told me not to worry, that there was probably nothing wrong.''

''You see?'' Della gave Caroline's hand a final pat and stood up to head for the stove once more. ''This is just a case of Willow being Willow. You mark my words. She'll turn up in a couple of days like a new penny, bright and shiny as can be. Now let me freshen that cup of yours."

Caroline accepted with a nod of thanks. Maybe she was on the wrong track after all. Della might be a bit absentminded sometimes, but she had never been stupid or dishonest. If she said that Willow was in the habit of making occasional short-term getaways, Caroline had no doubt that was the case. But why was her version of Willow's marriage so different from Willow's own?

"By the way, who did you talk to down at the police station?" Della asked. "Might it have been that nice Schaeffer boy?"

Caroline couldn't help smiling. That nice Schaeffer boy had to be a year or two over forty now.

"As I recall, once upon a time, you had something of an eye for him."

Caroline smiled wider. Della might not be so absentminded after all. "What made you remember that?"

"I never forget the important things," Della said, smoothing her apron before she sat down again. "He and his wife broke up, you know. She moved out of town and hasn't been much heard from since. I couldn't understand it myself, him being the real solid, upstanding type and all. And so good-looking, too. Don't you agree?"

Caroline didn't miss the direction of Della's inquisitiveness. The woman was in the preliminary stages of a matchmaking attempt, which Caroline definitely had to nip in the bud.

"Beauty is in the eye of the beholder, you always used to say. I'm afraid that Mr. Schaeffer is a little less than beautiful in my eyes."

"I see," Della said slowly. "And why would that be?"

"He thinks like too many of the men up here, that's all."

"I see," Della said again. "You always have been pretty hard on us north country folks, haven't you?"

"Have I?" Caroline was taken aback. Della had never criticized her before.

"Maybe you should give us more of a chance than you do. We're a hardworking lot, and keeping your nose to the grindstone can make you miss out on things once in a while. But there's no harm meant. You know how bad it used to make you feel when people made harsh judgments of you. You sure you want to be the one doing the judging?"

Della's warm smile made Caroline suddenly self-conscious. Della was referring to Caroline's mother and reminding, in a kind and caring way, that hers wasn't the example to be following. Perhaps she did need to rethink some of her opinions. But she was certain that her conclusions about Mike Schaeffer were correct. Luckily, Della didn't mention him again.

After leaving the house on St. Mary Street, Caroline decided to stop at a pay phone to call the Fowler summer cottage. Maybe Willow was there after all. The phone rang a few times before it was picked up.

"Willow, is that you?" a voice on the other end of the line said.

Caroline recognized it to be Justin, and he sounded sincerely worried. She hung up the receiver as quietly as she could manage. She had her answer. Unfortunately, she still had too many questions.

In her car once more, she found herself headed in the direction of the Burrville house. But she knew Willow wasn't there, nor were any clues to her whereabouts. Caroline reluctantly used a side road to turn around and had begun the drive back to her hotel when she heard the sound.

This time there could be no mistaking that it was a motorcycle, especially when she looked in the rearview mirror and saw the cycle approaching fast from behind. She told herself not to overreact, to distance herself from the influence of Willow's hysteria.

She maintained her original speed. The biker would be able to pass her easily on this road. She watched his approach in the mirror and refused to be alarmed by it.

Still, she couldn't help noticing how sinister he appeared in the near dusk, dressed in black leather with a black helmet and visor over his face; in fact, he could have been a woman as far as Caroline could tell. The rider leaned forward over the handlebars as if urging the big bike ever faster and straight toward Caroline's rear bumper.

He was getting close now and should be starting his move out into the other lane to pass, but Caroline saw no signs of any such move until what she judged must be the last possible moment. Then he pulled out just far enough to ride alongside her car.

The roar of the cycle engine was deafening, and she could feel its heat and smell the fumes through her partly opened window. She thought she heard a laugh, as well, deep and menacing, but that had to have been her imagination. The engine was so loud that no other sound was likely to penetrate the wall of noise.

Laugh or not, the menace was clear. Caroline's foot hit the accelerator, and the car sped forward, leaving cycle and cyclist in its wake. But only for a few moments. Then he began gaining on her again.

They were traveling well over the speed limit, but the motorcycle continued its chase. Caroline looked around for help but found none even as she neared the town.

She screeched into the first street that would lead to the center of the town, certain that traffic would intervene and force their headlong race to a halt. She no longer had any doubt that she was being pursued. The biker was still on her trail. Several pedestrians turned to watch as they sped past.

He stopped pursuing her as she reached the fork that led to the police station. He abruptly turned off into one of the side streets. Caroline continued to drive as fast as the increased traffic would allow for the remaining few blocks to the municipal building, then skidded the yellow car over the short incline into the parking lot.

The motor had barely ceased before Caroline shoved the car door open and scrambled out. She was hurrying across the parking lot when strong hands gripped her shoulders from behind.

Chapter Five

Caroline began to fight the moment she was grabbed. She struggled with all her might to free herself, and despite the much superior strength of her attacker, her sudden fierceness allowed her to wrench one arm from his grasp. She was about to jab him her very hardest shot with her elbow when she realized, through her rage, that she knew the voice that was trying to get her attention.

"It's me!" he was saying as she continued to fight him. "Caro, it's Mike!"

The words and their significance came together just in time to check the force of her jab somewhat but not completely. Her elbow struck him a glancing blow. She heard him grunt in surprise.

"Oh, Mike!" she cried, still out of breath from her struggles. "I'm sorry. I didn't know it was you. I thought it was the guy who was chasing me."

Mike turned her around to face him. "Who was chasing you?" he asked.

"I don't know who he was! He was riding a motorcycle and wearing a helmet that covered his face."

Caroline had kept herself under control during the ordeal of the pursuit. Panic had been with her in the yellow car all the way from Burrville Road, but she had not given in to it. She had shoved the terror down inside her while she did her best to save herself.

Now she was safe. She could see that safety in Mike's caring eyes and feel it in his strong hands. He wouldn't let anything or anyone harm her. He wouldn't even let her own legs collapse under her as they were threatening to do.

Tears of anger and relief rose in her throat. "He was all in black. I couldn't see him," she managed to say before the sobs began. "He wouldn't leave me alone. He wouldn't stop chasing me."

She tried desperately to regain her usual control, but it was too late. The flood of emotions she had held in check through the high-speed flight came tumbling forth.

She began to tremble violently, and Mike pulled her against him and enfolded her in his arms.

"Everything is all right now," he whispered in the gentlest voice she had ever heard. "Nobody can hurt you now. I'm here with you."

He kept one arm tightly around her as she reached up with the other to smooth her hair back from her face. Her tears caught it against her cheeks, and his fingers stroked the dampness away in a soothing rhythm as he rocked her slowly in his arms to calm her. He might have been a loving parent reassuring his child against the fears of the night. Through her turmoil, Caroline knew that never in her life had she felt as truly cared for as she did at this very moment.

"No one will hurt you," he crooned. "I won't let them."

A warning pierced the jumble of Caroline's emotions. She was still trembling but no longer so violently that she couldn't hear another kind of tremble in his voice. In a way, that tremble and what it suggested frightened her more than an entire squadron of black-clad pursuers might have done, and now her teeth began to chatter.

"You're freezing!" Mike said, chafing her upper arms with his broad, warm palms. "Let's get you inside," he said, guiding her toward the building. "Then I want to know exactly what happened to you tonight."

"Not in there," she said, resisting his guidance. Right now, she felt too exposed and vulnerable to bear the cold fluorescent glare of the police station.

"All right," he said. "Why don't we sit in my car." He did not question her seeming capriciousness but led the way to a nondescript sedan, which she assumed to be a police vehicle. Once inside, he gave her his jacket to put on and turned on the car heater. She almost wished his arms were still around her, but she knew that that way led danger.

"For a minute there," he mused aloud, "you reminded me of something. That night when you stayed over at our house with my sister."

Caroline could feel herself warming, and not from the heater. Why did he have to bring that up now?

"I've been thinking about that night ever since I first saw you in the hotel the other evening," he began. "It feels like...unfinished business between us."

That he was as awkward with the subject as she felt made her a little less nervous somehow. "I was just a foolish young girl with a crush on an older man," she said. "I'm the one who should be embarrassed, not you."

She patted his arm reassuringly, then was startled when he grasped her hand. "I'm not embarrassed," he said, leaning toward her and speaking intently. "It's simply very important to me that you understand what happened that night—and since then, too. You weren't the only one with an infatuation that couldn't go anywhere."

Now Caroline was the one who couldn't think what to say. He had released her hand, and she stared at where it rested on the seat between them.

"When I was married," he went on, "my wife once accused me of carrying a torch for you."

"You told your wife about me?" she said in astonishment.

"I told her everything. We were the best of friends. Too bad we weren't much more than that or maybe we would have stayed together. She was right about your being special to me. After those years in Nam, it felt to me like you must be the only sweet, pure thing left in the world."

Caroline heard the plaintive note in his deep voice, and tears rose to her eyes. She wanted to take him in her arms and comfort him, but she didn't dare. Her own feelings were even more chaotic than his.

"I could tell you were very troubled by whatever happened to you over there," she said.

He pulled himself back up straight, as if suddenly realizing he had revealed too much. "I keep all of that over and done and in the past."

"I see," said Caroline. Any number of veterans of that war, she knew, had had to find ways of dealing with its demons. Many chose repression.

"I'm not sure how much of what I felt for you then had to do with the war," said Mike, once again seeming to struggle for words and understanding. "But I do want you to know I understand that that was then and this is now."

"What do you mean by that?" she asked, already dismayed by what she sensed he was about to say.

"I mean," he continued, "that once upon a time you had a fantasy, and I had one, too, and they happened to get mixed into each other for a while."

As his words sank in, Caroline sat up straight, as well. He had made himself very clear indeed. He had let her know in unequivocal terms that his recent attentions to her had been in deference to a poignant but distant interlude, which he remembered with affection but little more. So why wasn't she pleased? She had had no intention of caring about some narrow-minded north country male herself.

"You are absolutely right about that," she said, and she supposed she believed what she was saying. "Of course, we can still be friends."

"Very good friends, I hope," he said quietly.

That sealed it for sure, since this was one man who clearly understood the difference between friendship and romance between a man and woman. His marriage had taught him that.

"Now that you've had a chance to calm down," he said, suddenly his usual cool and casual self once more, "let's talk about what happened to you tonight."

So that was why he had brought up their past. To distract her for a while until she composed herself enough to be questioned. She had employed the technique herself on occasion with distraught clients at the therapy center. Mike deserved compliments on his proficiency, but she wasn't about to offer them.

"I was chased for several miles by someone on a motorcycle," she said.

Mike reached toward her, and she was so startled that she made a small jump away from him.

"I need my notebook and pen," he said. "They're in my jacket pocket."

"Oh, yes," she said, pulling her arms hastily out of the sleeves. "I'd forgotten I had it on."

"You can keep it. I just need the notebook."

"Oh, no. I don't need this anymore," she said, practically tossing the jacket at him. "I'm plenty warm enough now, thank you."

In truth, she was uncomfortably so, especially in the area of her cheeks. She was also aware of sounding much more flustered than she preferred.

"Did you happen to notice the license plate or make of the motorcycle or anything else distinctive about it?" Mike asked as he fished a small notebook out of the jacket and opened it.

"I didn't see the license plate, but I think the bike was a Harley, one of the bigger models." Caroline was determined to come across as one hundred percent the intelligent professional for the rest of this interview.

"What do you remember about the driver?" Mike was obviously just as intent about staying strictly business as he scribbled notations in his pad.

"Medium height. Medium build. Black leather jacket and gloves. Black helmet with opaque visor. Probably dark jeans and boots, but I couldn't say for sure about that," she said.

Mike stopped scribbling and looked at her with some interest. "Could it possibly have been a woman?"

"I don't think so."

Caroline was beginning to feel irritated. She realized it had more to do with what had gone on between them before than with the questions he was asking now, but whatever her motivation, she dearly wished this interview she had sought would come to an end quickly.

Her impatience was apparent in her voice. "What I do think is that whoever chased me has something to do with Willow's disappearance." It frustrated her still more to remember that Mike didn't believe Willow was missing in the first place.

"Why do you think that?" he asked.

"Because Willow was convinced that somebody on a bike was chasing us last night when I drove her to—when I was driving her home."

Caroline hadn't told him where she had taken Willow. Knowing that Willow had stayed at some man's house would only strengthen his doubts about her.

"Did you actually see a motorcycle following you last night?" he asked.

"No, but I may have heard one."

"But you can't say definitely whether you did or not."

"No, I can't."

"But Willow was sure there was a biker after you?"

"That's right."

"I see" was Mike's only reply.

He hadn't written any of what she'd said in his pad. She could tell he didn't believe her. She supposed she couldn't blame him, really. After talking with Della earlier and then hearing Justin's supposedly worried voice on the phone, Caroline almost hadn't believed in the menace Willow feared, either. However, since being chased, she had changed her mind. Again she wondered about the biker outside her hotel that night, but in the face of Mike's irritating disbelief, she kept a lid on her thoughts, refusing to be labeled a skittish female suspecting everyone.

"Any chance the biker who chased you just now could have been Willow?"

"What?" His question had come from so far out of left field that Caroline's mouth fell open.

"It's remotely possible the person on the cycle could have been a woman. And if so, that woman could have been Willow Fowler."

"What a bizarre thing to suggest," Caroline said, not even trying to hide her exasperation.

"You're right." Mike slapped the notebook shut. "You'll have to excuse my policeman's brain. Sometimes I can't shut it off from making suspicious connections. But, more realistically, this biker chasing you was probably a case of horny hormones run wild. You have to remember that you're an attractive woman driving a yellow sports car," Mike said as he returned the notebook to his pocket. "I don't know how that affects the men where you come from, but up here it can get you some attention you may not want."

Something about the way he said that zinged the wire of Caroline's irritation taut and twanging. Or maybe it was the way his flipping that notebook shut had sent the unmistakable message that, as far as he was concerned, she had nothing to say that he could take seriously enough to write down.

"That isn't what happened," she snapped. "And if you aren't smart enough to see that, I am."

"I'm afraid that I have to depend on facts first and intuition afterward."

He was using his gentle, calming voice again, and that only antagonized Caroline more. "Well, how very nice for you," she said, very caustically, as she jabbed the door handle downward and pushed open the door.

"Caro, I didn't mean to upset you about this. I'll check up on Willow as soon as I get a chance, and I'll let you know whatever I find out."

Caroline was out of the car, about to close the door. She leaned down and looked in at him to reply coldly, "Why don't you just do that."

She slammed the door and marched away, aware that she was being bad-tempered and maybe even a bit unreasonable.

THEY HAD FOUND the body. It was on the late-night news. Must have been on the earlier broadcast, too. There were the police, walking around the place, not letting anybody past the ropes they had put up, just like in the movies. Except that this wasn't a murder case. This was an accident.

An accident is something that happens even though nobody planned it that way. Nobody had planned for him to call up after so many years and say he was in town. The place they met had been specially picked so nothing could possibly go wrong.

They would get together. He would get his money or whatever he was after, and then he would leave town. Nobody would know a thing about it, and nobody would connect either of them to their meeting place. Everything had been planned out in detail.

Then things began to go wrong.

First of all, there shouldn't have been that question right at the start, but the curiosity had been too much to bear.

"How did you find out so much about what I'm doing now?"

His eyes had shifted sideways in that sneaky way he always had. Then he'd sneered.

"You aren't smart enough to keep anything from me when I put my mind to finding it out. I got my ways." His eyes shifted off again, examining the room. "If you done as well for yourself as I hear, how come you don't have a fancier place than this?"

Thump. Thump. Whose heartbeat was that, getting faster all of a sudden? He could do that—upset a person just by being in the same room, sneering and talking in that snide tone of voice. It happened every time.

Still, there was something exciting about it happening now, the same way it had all those years ago, back when there was no way to get away from him yet. After all, this moment proved in a way that all those long-ago moments had actually taken place, and that they were really as bad as memory made them out to be.

"You probably don't have a drink around here, either," he said, slurring the words.

His goading drove the excitement up to throat level. He had said that on purpose to get a reaction. Mention of his drinking always did that. When he talked about it, there wasn't any way to pretend that it didn't exist or that he wasn't filthy and disgusting and violent when he did it. He was deliberately making everything like it used to be—horrible and inescapable. He was still the enemy and always would be, exactly as he had been all that time ago.

He staggered as he reached for the inside pocket of his rumpled raincoat. "I don't need your damned booze," he said. "I brought my own."

He dragged out a brown paper bag that was pressed and creased into the shape of a pint whiskey bottle. *Thump. Thump. Thump.* How much was a person supposed to be able to bear? He was still a nasty, sloppy drunk, and, worst of all, he was here, where he had no business being at all.

He leered over the ragged edge of the brown paper bag, then took a swig, tipping his head back to get his greedy fill while his Adam's apple bobbed up and down in his scrawny neck. "It's the good stuff, too. I always get the good stuff."

How much hatred was it possible to feel for a person before it exploded and tore you apart? There used to be the option of running out of the room and finding a cubbyhole to hide in, but that only worked for children. There were no cubbyholes big enough now. He had to be faced down this time, once and for all.

This time he had to be the one to turn tail and run and never come back again.

"Wha's wrong? Cat got your tongue?" he slurred. "Don't you want to know where I've been all these years?"

"There's no point in asking you anything. You'll only lie like you always have."

"I won't lie. I swear. Ask me whatever you want to know, and I'll tell you the God's honest truth."

Wait. He would never have said "God's honest truth" back then. He'd never believed in God, or anything else for that matter. Could he be a stranger after all? He did look different—grayer, more wrinkled. A lot more wrinkled. But his eyes couldn't belong to anybody else. There was no mistaking their mocking expression. It was him all right, and he had to be gotten rid of as fast as possible.

"All I want to know is what you're doing here now."

"What if I told you I'm here to get us back together again? What would you say to that?" He put a nasty twist on the way he said that so there was no chance of mistaking it for sincerity. "Don't you remember how you used to care so much about that togetherness stuff? You'd shut yourself up in your room and snivel about it for hours."

"I'm not sniveling now."

He flung his head up so the cords of his neck pulled taut. Then he laughed with a mean, cackling sound. Was that the same laugh from all those years ago? Suddenly the memories weren't as clear as they had been. Anger did that to a person, heated things up and confused you until it was hard to be clear anymore.

When he had finished laughing, he took another swig from the brown bag, almost choking on one last chuckle he apparently couldn't hold back. "I don't suppose somebody as high-toned as you has much call for sniveling these goddamned days."

"You talk like street trash. You used to have a little breeding. Now you don't even have that."

"Breeding?" He laughed again, more of a snort this time. "Who cares about breeding, except maybe that sainted mother of yours? She used to talk about that stuff, didn't she?"

"Don't you talk about my mother! I won't have her name dirtied by your speaking it."

The exhilaration of saying that was almost overwhelming. Years of angry words pressed against years of restraint, like floodwaters surging against a dam.

"There's a good reason for sticking around here," he said.

The gleam in his too-bright eyes was almost merry. Such eyes deserved nothing better than to be punched at until they swelled up too tight for even a glimmer to escape.

"I think I'll set myself up right here in this jerk-water town of yours," he said. "Then I can come around every day and talk to you about your dear old mom. Maybe I can even get together with the old girl again, bring her around here, too."

"You won't stay around here, and you won't talk to me about anything, and you won't go anywhere near my mother!"

Those angry feelings were slamming against the floodgate. There would be no holding them back much longer.

"I'll stay where I feel like staying, and I'll talk about what I damned well please with any damn body I want to."

"No, you will not!" The shout was so loud that if there had been anybody else around they surely would have heard. But at that time of night, the building was deserted. "I don't want to hear your filth again as long as I live!" That shout was louder still.

There hadn't been any thought of pushing him. It simply happened—one quick shove that caught him while he was raising the bottle again. He must have been off balance and couldn't keep himself from falling. His head hit the corner of the table with a dull thud. He dropped to the floor all at once, like dead weight.

He lay on the cheap tweed carpet, half on his side, with one arm flung across his chest. His grip had loosened, and the brown bag had slipped out of his hand, but there was no spill. His eyes were open wide as if he'd been surprised, and the sneer was gone from his lips.

Accident! Accident. Not my fault! Not my fault! The thoughts were so loud they screamed through the room.

So why were they on television now calling it a suspicious death? Why didn't they say he got drunk and fell down and hit his head? Can't they see that must be what happened? Why are they making so much fuss over an old drunk anyway?

This wasn't part of the plan. It had been a careful plan, and a good one, too. What could have gone wrong?

Then again, maybe nothing had gone wrong. Maybe the police were making a big a deal of this to get themselves some publicity. If that was the case, they would be doing more investigating. There was no telling what they might find out. They might even discover the truth.

Another plan was needed right away, and this one had to be foolproof. Every detail had to be worked out just right. There was no such thing as being too thorough in a situation like this. But what could that plan be?

There was no way to stop the investigation. But what about diverting it? What about creating a smoke screen that would cover up what had really happened and send them off looking in another direction? That could work.

But what could possibly distract the police from a dead body...? Except maybe another dead body!

Chapter Six

The next day began as a perfect autumn morning, except that it was July. Ordinarily, Caroline would have grumbled and shivered, but today she was grateful for the brisk air that snapped her head clear at the first whiff. This was just the kind of morning she needed to get her thoughts in order about what exactly could be going on around here. Unfortunately, when she did get those thoughts in line, they marched immediately out of control and straight in the direction of Mike Schaeffer. To her horror, she found herself wondering if he could ever find her attractive.

Appearance-wise, she knew what her strong points were. She had good legs. They were long and well shaped and firm enough that she didn't have to worry about going flabby soon. Still, she was not so sinewy that she looked like one of those morning jogging addicts she saw sprinting along the side roads back in Westchester, where word had not yet penetrated that the exercise-till-it-kills-you craze was past its prime.

She also had a fine complexion—what Della Gilchrist had always called "English skin," swept clear by centuries of cleansing rain and pinkened by a touch of salty sea breeze.

As a teen she had despaired of ever having a fashionably correct figure. Androgynous slenderness had been in forever, while she had both hips and breasts. But as an adult she recognized that curves were just fine—and that many men preferred them. She wondered if Mike was one of those men.

She also knew very well why she was concerning herself in the first place about what he might or might not prefer. More than once in the last couple of days she had been reminded of a man she saw a fair amount of a few years ago and why that relationship, along with several others like it, had not worked out. There simply had not been anything special enough about the guy for her to make a major commitment to him.

When she tried to explain that breakup to her friends, she knew she sounded very arbitrary in her judgment because she couldn't really put into words what that special something might be. Consequently, her friends had shaken their heads in despair of her ever finding a man to share her life with. Only Helena Blanchard, then in their beginning months as business partners, had seemed to understand what Caroline was talking about.

Yet, even with Helena, Caroline refrained from saying that she would recognize that special quality if and when she encountered it. That remark might have prompted disdain, as well as despair, maybe even from herself. Now, all of a sudden, she felt differently. Such a statement would be right on target for her reaction to Mike Schaeffer. Whatever conflicts they might have in other areas, she could sense that specialness emanating from him like heat waves radiating off a summer highway. Too bad there were conflicts between them nonetheless—big, important ones like towering stone walls too formidable to take on, much less surmount.

Also too bad was Caroline's feeling that she had to do Mike's job for him where Willow was concerned. As Caroline saw it, his macho attitudes had narrowed his mind so much that he couldn't recognize what was right in front of his face—the possibility that something bad could have happened to Willow. The police were supposed to involve themselves with possible crimes as well as probable ones. Yet, Mike wasn't doing a thing when the circumstances obviously—to Caroline's way of thinking anyway—cried out for something to be done.

Which meant that she had no choice. Part of her, perhaps the part that included her common sense, cried out just as loudly for her to get herself out of this situation and back to her own life where she belonged. Still, a voice from another quarter was not to be denied. She imagined that voice to originate in the direction of her conscience, insisting that she do what she knew in her heart was right. She had to make airtight certain that Willow was all right now and that she would be free to make her own choices in the future. After Caroline had assured herself of that, she would finally and gratefully leave the north country behind, including Mike Schaeffer and the disappointment that her reunion with him had turned out to be.

Caroline considered her plan of action. Visit the scene, she told herself. She had already been to the place where Willow was supposed to be—the Burrville house. What about the scene of what Willow alleged to be her problematic life? What about the big house on Flower Avenue West that she and Justin called home? Caroline didn't debate her next move any further. She headed for her car.

Willow's house was only a few blocks from the hotel. Caroline recalled that Justin had wanted to live in one of the newer, more currently fashionable areas, like Schley Drive or Sunset Ridge, but Willow had insisted on Flower Avenue West. She had stood her ground on that point with a determination very unlike her usual pliant nature. Apparently, even Justin had been impressed because, in this instance at least, Willow got her way.

Caroline understood her friend's insistence on this point. When they were both growing up here, the gracious, stately houses of what she thought of as the Ives Hill section of town, near the country club of that name, had stood for something. They represented a gentility of life as staunch as the tall, broad trees that shaded them and as pervasive and far-reaching as the root systems running beneath. Much of the concrete evidence of that life was gone now. Many of the old families had scattered. Some had all but faded out. Even the great houses Caroline and Willow had loved and fantasized about were too often now only suggestions of what they used to be.

Caroline noted with sadness their peeling paint and neglected shrubbery as she drove along. She knew very well that huge houses like these were as obsolete as the dinosaur. They were too expensive to maintain. They didn't suit today's smaller families and more hurried lives. They had been built with hired help in mind as a given in the daily lives of those who lived in them. None of that applied to the lives of today, especially in a remotely located small city whose population had been dwindling over the years along with its productivity and net worth. Caroline understood Willow's determination to put up at least one bulwark against consigning to oblivion this world of their adolescent fantasies.

Of course, the Fowler house showed no signs of deterioration or neglect. The paint was fresh and white and gleamed in the sun, with black shutters to accentuate the wide-paned windows across both stories of the broad front. A very old, very substantial oak tree commanded the front lawn, which stretched the width of two or more ordinary lots. Off to the side, near the screened-in porch, stood a tall blue spruce. Caroline could imagine how wonderful that evergreen must smell on a truly autumnal day.

Today, however, the air was perfumed by the deep flower beds that bordered the house with a splash of colors and profusion of blossoms. At times like this Caroline wished she knew a bit less about business and a bit more about outdoor things, like horticulture. She would bet that Willow knew the name and nature of every one of those blossoms. Willow had always loved beautiful and delicate things, and her touch and taste were as unmistakably represented by these flower beds as if her signature had been etched upon the soil.

Suddenly Caroline knew with more certainty than ever that the things she had heard suggested about Willow these past few days—that she was a careless, frivolous woman who played fast and loose with her marital vows—simply didn't ring true. She might not

be on a career fast track, but Caroline of all people
knew that having different goals didn't make them
lesser goals.

Willow was a lady in the old-fashioned sense, a
preserver of what was gracious and lovely and tradi-
tional. That would hold true at least as much for
marriage as for old houses and flower gardens! Caroline was virtually convinced of that. Though her
conviction originated in an area of her consciousness
that just-the-facts-ma'am Mike Schaeffer might scoff
at as less than logical, Caroline approached the grand
white house feeling more surely that she was on the
right path to get to the truth than she had since her
arrival in Watertown.

She hesitated only briefly out front. The yellow
sports car stuck out like a sore thumb parked by the
low curb on the wide street. It occurred to Caroline
that she might not want to be so conspicuous. It also
occurred to her that she was thinking in cloak-and-
dagger terms, but, following her instincts, she pulled
the car into the driveway and around toward the car
park strategically placed so as not to detract from the
head-on prospect of this showplace house.

The door onto the screened porch area was open.
The furniture was white with soft chintz cushions in a
pattern that picked up the warm tone of the terra-cotta
floor. There were glass tables here and there bearing
current magazines and several large-format art and
photography books.

Caroline could imagine Willow poring over those
coffee-table books, and savoring aesthetic beauty.
How many times in high school had Caroline found
Willow sitting on the floor in the back stacks of the li-

brary doing exactly that with some art book or another. Suddenly Caroline missed her friend very much
and wished they were sitting together right now among
these chintz cushions, talking and laughing the way
they had always loved to do.

She rapped on the door into the main house. She
waited a few seconds and rapped again.

Nobody responded.

She hesitated only briefly before trying the door.
When the knob turned easily, she didn't hesitate for
long before stepping inside. She was reminded of how
north country people would most likely lock the front
door but might not be so cautious about the others,
especially in the more casual summer season.

The interior of the house reflected the same comfortable elegance as the screened porch had. Willow
had had excellent taste even when she was a girl; marriage to Justin had given her the means to exercise that
taste, and the result was most pleasing.

In addition, Caroline thought, Justin got the perfect home for an ambitious man out to make a good
impression. Willow had said he kept her coiffed and
dressed to suit his image. Caroline had wondered at
Willow's attitude then, but now she was beginning to
suspect otherwise.

"Is anybody home?" Caroline called out, a bit uneasy about being well inside a house she had not been
invited to enter.

When there was no answer, she moved to the main
hallway and called out more loudly. The grand stair-
case was nearby. She decided to check upstairs for
signs of Willow's whereabouts, since there didn't appear to be anyone here to direct otherwise. Never be-

fore in Caroline's life had she snuck into someone's house in their absence and proceeded to search the place, yet in less than three full days she was already guilty of two such trespasses. Upstate seemed to be bringing out the criminal in her.

The stairs were carpeted in an authentic Chinese weave. Obviously no expense had been spared in this household. No wonder Della Gilchrist, who'd had to make do with little, was happy with Justin as Willow's husband.

Della's generation believed one of the best things a man could be was a good provider. But Caroline knew Willow well enough to understand that authentic Chinese carpeting would not be enough to make her happy. A husband would need to provide for her spirit, not just her senses, as she would most certainly do for him in return. Caroline's instincts suggested that such mutual emotional sustenance might not be abundant in the Fowler marriage.

She was at the top of the stairs and about to begin trying doorknobs when she heard the sound. It came from downstairs and could have been a door closing. Her heart fluttered. She stole a quick glance over the bannister but saw no one. She thought she heard somebody moving around but couldn't be sure. Of course, the carpeting would muffle footsteps. Or she could be imagining things. She was certainly keyed up enough. Creeping around other people's houses on the sly was definitely not her cup of tea.

She heard another door close somewhere below, and that unsettled her even more. Better to be fantasizing alarming noises than to be caught in the act of criminal trespass. That possibility kept her from calling out to establish her presence, as she would have under more normal circumstances. Instead, she backed against the nearest doorway, where she couldn't be seen from the lower hall.

She wasn't expecting the door to open behind her, and when it did, she almost screamed. She spun around, but no one was there. She was alone in a room bright enough to be startling in itself. She must have pushed the door open herself without meaning to.

This had to be Willow's sewing room. Ruffled white curtains shimmered in the sunlight from the bay windows. There were books and magazines in a brass-banded bucket next to a cushioned rocker, and a small writing table, as well. A state-of-the-art sewing machine was bathed in light from yet another window, and the nearby dress form corresponded to Willow's feminine proportions. In fact, the room itself reminded Caroline of Willow, more strongly than any of those downstairs.

But there was no time to think about that now. Caroline found what she needed right next to the sewing machine. The shears were long and thin, the point sharp enough to make a treacherous weapon. She grasped the shears firmly and moved back to the door, which she had left partly opened.

Whomever she had heard beyond the bannister was now coming up the stairs. Maybe it was Justin, or even Willow. Caroline told herself that she was probably behaving like a fool. What if Justin or Willow found her here clutching a pair of shears like some kind of crazed murderess? Caroline would rather they thought of her as a nosy intruder than a maniac. Again, she almost called out, "Hello. Who's there?" but something stopped her.

The sound of the footsteps on the stairs wasn't right somehow. She listened intently. They were moving very slowly, one step at a time, as if with great caution. Would a person climb the stairs that way in his or her own house? Caroline didn't think so. A few moments ago she had come up those same stairs just as slowly and cautiously. She had done that because she didn't belong here. She had a strong feeling this person didn't belong here, either.

She clutched the shears all the more tightly in front of her and flattened her back against the wall next to the door opening. The footsteps had reached the top of the stairs and proceeded to a point just beyond where she stood. She heard a slight thump there and wondered if whoever it was might have done the same thing. That would mean the two of them were standing back to back, with only the thickness of the wall between them.

Caroline willed herself not to move. Maybe whoever it was didn't know she was here. The slightest sound could alert him to her presence. Still, she had her weapon ready if he did come through the door. She told herself she wouldn't hesitate to use that weapon if she had to, but her heart was pounding so hard and her breath pinched so thin that she wondered it she would be too frightened to strike when the time came to do so. Till this moment, she hadn't been aware of how chilly the wall was beneath its bright, cheery paper.

She eased her shoulder blades away, and in that instant she sensed a movement on the other side of the wall. She tensed, ready to spring if need be. Still, she wasn't prepared for the steel muzzle of a pistol that appeared in the doorway. She couldn't take her eyes off it as she quickly raised her own weapon on high.

"Caro, don't! It's me!"

She had already begun her lunge with the shears when she looked up to see Mike Schaeffer making a grab for her wrist. The sharp, narrow point was only inches short of his chest when together they checked her thrust. He held on to her wrist for a moment, perhaps making certain she had actually comprehended his identity. He was looking down at her as if he might be seeing that crazy murderess she had thought about what now seemed like eons ago.

"Let go of me," she protested, pulling futilely against his grasp, her teeth gritted with the effort.

"Take it easy," he said in a low-pitched, even voice as if disarming an overwrought criminal.

Exasperated that he might lump her together with such a type made Caroline tug all the harder.

"You let go of me this second or I am going to kick you so hard you won't know what hit you," she growled with a vehemence that surprised even her.

He stepped back instinctively without letting go of her wrist. Then he glanced down at her feet, and, to Caroline's total undoing, he began to laugh.

"In that case, I'm glad those aren't exactly hob-nailed boots you have on," he said with that galling chuckle.

Caroline looked down, at her feet as well, and saw instantly what he meant. She had regretted wearing sandals as soon as she stepped outside the hotel this morning and found the weather cool again despite the sun mounting gradually in the sky. She had considered going back inside to change but was in too much of a hurry to get here to Willow's house. Besides, she had welcomed the bracing chill that would keep her nerves sharp for the sleuthing she had in mind.

The chance of needing to enlist her toe as deliverer of a well placed kick simply had not occurred to her. The narrow leather thongs encircling that toe at this moment could hardly be capable of inflicting much damage. Her coral pink toenail polish made the prospect even more ludicrous. Caroline relaxed her grip on the shears at the thought as a chuckle of her own rose in her throat.

"See what I mean?" asked Mike. He relaxed his grip on her wrist, as well.

"Yes, I do." She couldn't help but shake her head in wonder at her own behavior. She wasn't the type to go around threatening people with bodily harm.

He didn't release her arm altogether, but he had slipped the gun behind his belt. Now he took the shears away from her gently, set them on a nearby table and began to massage the place where he had held her so tightly only moments ago.

"I hope I didn't hurt you," he said.

He spoke gently, but Caroline sensed this was no longer his professional calm-the-perp voice. She thought she heard something much more personal there, and the stroke of his fingers against the sensitive skin of her wrist was hardly putting her at ease.

"I'm sorry I nearly stabbed you," she said as lightly as she could manage, given the turmoil of the last several minutes. "You'd better be careful not to take me by surprise too often."

"I've had to learn that lesson twice now," he said. "Believe me, I won't need a third demonstration."

He was smiling down at her, and they were standing only inches apart. She was looking straight into his gray eyes, noticing the dark flecks there that she had never been close enough to see before.

His lips had curved up at the corners, but that smile began to fade as he returned her gaze. And suddenly she could almost feel his lips on hers, though neither of them had moved. And with great clarity she knew that there was nothing in heaven or earth she wanted more right now than to have him pull her against him, close the inches between them and smother her mouth with his.

She let out a trembling gasp. How could this man's gaze so readily pierce her defenses and create such intense sensations? With the remnant of willpower she had left, Caroline pushed herself away from him and retrieved her wrist from the hypnotic stroking of his fingers.

The feelings were too strong. They were sweeping her away. She had to think.

"What are you doing here?" she at last.

"I came to make good on my promise to you." The rasp in his voice traveled along her already ravaged nerves like a searing flame, suggesting all manner of sensual promises. "I came to find out what has happened to Willow Fowler."

Chapter Seven

"I thought you didn't believe anything *had* happened to Willow," Caroline said, her senses still awhirl.

"When a responsible citizen comes to me with a suspicion or complaint, I always take it seriously. I'm sorry to say that last evening some other considerations got in the way of my judgment."

"What other considerations?"

"I think you know."

Mike's gaze locked with hers again, but she wasn't about to fall under his spell a second time. Besides, was he talking about her or about the call he'd received?

"I take it you have now decided to consider the source of this particular suspicion," she said.

"Yes, I have."

"And what is your verdict?"

"I don't think you're the type of woman who would do something as drastic as making a complaint to the police if you didn't believe something was seriously wrong."

"Maybe I was just trying to get to see you." The minute she made that very flip comment, she wondered why she had done it and wished she hadn't.

"I may be mistaken, but that doesn't strike me as your style." He hadn't taken on her flipness. He sounded almost solemn.

"You're right. I'm not," she said. "It isn't my style to overreact or imagine trouble where it doesn't exist."

"That's why I decided to pursue this thing for you. That and because I told you I would."

"So you decided to search her house?"

"Hardly. I could only do that if I had probable cause and a warrant, which I don't. I only came in because the door was ajar, and I thought there might be somebody inside who wasn't quite so concerned about legalities as I am." He gazed at her evenly.

Caroline shrugged. "I know I shouldn't have come in uninvited, but no one answered the door, and I was sincerely afraid for Willow and what must have happened to her. At the moment, that seemed more important than anything else."

What seemed most important right now was getting out of here. Caroline moved into the hallway and headed for the stairs. Mike followed.

When they reached the living room, Caroline nearly gasped at finding a strange woman staring at them with some surprise.

"Hello, Martha. How are you?" Mike said easily. He didn't appear at all ruffled to be discovered uninvited on somebody else's private property.

"I'm fair to middlin', Michael. Though you gave me a bit of a fright comin' down those stairs like that when nobody's supposed to be at home,'' Martha said, looking more skeptically at Caroline than at him.

"Miss Hardin here is an old friend of Mrs. Fowler's,'' Mike said. "She's been trying to get in touch with Willow and hasn't been able to. She was afraid something might have happened to her.''

"That's right,'' Martha said, finally favoring Caroline with a smile. "You called here yesterday morning, and I told you that Mrs. Fowler had gone off on one of her little trips. She does that sometimes.''

"Did she tell you she was going or where she would be?''

"No, she didn't, but she doesn't always. My guess is it makes her feel more free and easy to think she can come and go as she pleases without reportin' in to anybody.''

Martha's tone suggested she didn't approve of such an attitude, though she was careful not to overstep her bounds by coming right out and saying so. But, more important, she was suggesting essentially the same thing Della Gilchrist had.

"What makes you so certain she's taken one of those trips this time?'' Mike asked.

"She packed up a bag just like always.''

"How do you know she did that?''

Mike was really pursuing this. Caroline was impressed by that, but she also suspected that Martha was a dead end.

"There's a suitcase and some of her clothes missing,'' Martha said, obviously proud to be so knowledgeable about the details of her employer's life.

"Do you have any idea where Mrs. Fowler goes when she makes trips like this?'' Mike asked.

"I got no idea where she goes—or who she goes with, either, for that matter." There could be no mistaking Martha's disapproval now. "All I know is that she's gone a few days, then she comes back no worse for wear. Fact is, she generally comes back lookin' like she's had herself a good old time."

To Caroline, Martha's implication was clear. She thought that Willow was in the habit of making the occasional sojourn with a man, or men, other than her husband. That was something like what Justin had supposedly told Mike. Nonetheless, if Mike had any bias in that direction, he gave no sign of it.

"Mind if I butt in for a moment?" Caroline asked.

Martha was looking as if she definitely did mind, but Caroline didn't let that stop her.

"Did you work for Mr. Fowler before he got married?"

"I most certainly did. I have worked for Mr. Fowler ever since he first moved to town."

"What did you think about his marrying Willow Gilchrist?"

Martha's eyes widened in surprise at the question. The expression that crossed her face next answered that question more plainly than words could ever have done. She didn't approve of Willow as a wife for Justin Fowler any more than she approved of Willow's friend being here asking nosy questions.

"I'm the housekeeper here, miss. That's all. I got no business thinking anything one way or the other about what Mr. Fowler does," Martha said. "Is there anything else I can help you with?" Martha made a point of addressing this last to Mike.

"Unless there's something else Miss Hardin would like to know, I'd say that's all we need right now."

"Nothing further," Caroline said.

For one thing, she had found out that Willow had no ally in the woman who kept house for her. She hoped Mike had made the same observation and would consider Martha's comments accordingly.

They had left the house, and Caroline was about to make that suggestion to Mike when he made an intriguing suggestion of his own.

"I think it's time we had a talk with Justin about all this."

"Does that mean you think something could have happened to Willow after all?"

"All it means is that Justin is a major player in this little drama, and we need to hear his side of the story. How well do you know him anyway?"

"Actually, I hardly know him at all. I met him at the wedding, and the three of us went out to dinner once when he and Willow visited New York together. That's all."

"What about when you visited here?"

"I haven't been back here since Willow's wedding."

"Why is that?"

Caroline wasn't as comfortable with that question as she would have liked to be. "I thought we were talking about Willow, not about me," she said.

"Sorry." Mike's grin was disarming. "Cops are nosy by nature, you know."

"As I said, I hardly know Justin," she said. "I never even saw their house till today. They hadn't bought it yet at the time of the wedding."

"There was a lot of talk when they did, about how Willow wanted to play lady of the manor by setting herself up in a huge old relic like that."

"Willow doesn't think that way at all," Caroline snapped. "Tell me. Is it also a cop's nature to listen to small-minded gossip?"

Mike studied her for a moment. "Only if there's some truth in it," he said.

"There isn't. Now, let's get back to Justin. I assume you'd like me to tell you what kind of impression he made on me the few times I met him."

"That might be interesting."

He's amused by this, Caroline thought. She vowed to keep cool as a cucumber and not let her growing irritation show.

"He was very charming," she said. "Extremely charming as a matter of fact. Maybe too much so."

"This extremely charming type of man—am I right in concluding they aren't your personal favorites?"

Caroline didn't answer that. She wasn't about to give him the satisfaction of knowing how close he had come to the truth.

"In which case," he went on, his grin still intact, "I can't understand why you're not absolutely bowled over by me. I don't have an ounce of charm in my entire body."

Caroline decided to avoid the subject of Mike's personality and how it might or might not affect her.

"I think you're right about paying Justin a visit," she said. "Can we do that now?"

"Only if you bribe me with lunch first."

He was smiling at her in a way that made her heart forget her irritation with him. She felt the old confusion returning. Was he simply trying to be friends, as he'd suggested last night in the police station parking lot, or had the incident in Willow's sewing room affected him as much as it had her? She had no way of telling from his offhand manner. She decided it might be wise to behave likewise for now.

"I would have thought that bribes were out of the question for a good cop," she said.

"Even a good cop has his price," he said. "Lunch just might be it for me. What do you say?"

Caroline could hardly have been more relieved when the sound of Mike's beeper rescued her from the need to answer him. He walked to his car, which was parked in front of the Fowler's house. That would explain why he hadn't known she was inside. From here he couldn't have seen her small car.

When Mike headed back toward Caroline a few minutes later, his former offhandedness had disappeared. The strong features that made him more handsome and manly than Caroline cared to admit had tensed into something much harder yet just as appealing. Dangerously so.

"What's happened?" she asked.

"Another body has been found," he said absently, as if he hardly remembered she was there.

"You mean like the one the other night down by the river?"

"That's right, except this one was found up by the cider mill," Mike said, still musing aloud rather than talking to her.

"The cider mill?"

"That's right."

Mike had turned to go back to his car. Caroline darted after him. "Do you mind if I follow you out there?" she asked.

"To the mill? Why?"

"I have my reasons. Please don't say no."

Mike nodded, looking only somewhat quizzical. Caroline guessed that he would hardly have consented so readily if he were less distracted. She headed toward her car before he could change his mind and start questioning her more closely. She didn't care to tell him that the place where this body had been found was only a quarter of a mile down the road from the house where she had last seen Willow two nights ago.

THE SUN DAPPLED DOWN through the trees into spots of light and shadow, drifting this way and that with the gentle movement of the leaves in the breeze. The beauty of the scene was out of sync with what Mike had come to see.

The body was largely unbloodied, like the other one. Yet there was a break in the scalp where a blow had fallen. They found no bottle in a brown bag this time, but the old man reeked of whiskey as strongly as if he were still able to breathe it out into the air around him.

One more difference from the first John Doe Mike noted immediately. Palumbo was the one to acknowledge it out loud.

"We won't have any problem ID-ing this one," he said.

"Yeah," Mike agreed with a sigh. "It's Smokey Rhodes."

Everybody on the force knew Smokey. He had spent so many nights sleeping off a drunk in the county jail that they had stopped keeping records on it a long time ago. They didn't even call it an arrest anymore. Picking Smokey up was referred to as putting him in protective custody to avoid paperwork. Mike stared down at the old man's gray, rigid face and wished the city had been protecting him last night, as well.

"So what do you think?" asked Palumbo.

"What do *you* think? You got here first."

"Well, it comes to mind that this place is a long way from home for old Smokey."

"Exactly."

Smokey had a run-down furnished room on Court Street. Mike had taken him there once when he seemed sober enough not to need the city lockup to make it through the night. The place had been typical of its occupant—swaybacked narrow bed in the corner with a threadbare spread thrown over it, ancient black-and-white TV set with a wire clothes hanger for an antenna, scarred dresser with a two-burner hot plate on top that was against the landlord's so-called house rules.

Smokey had no relatives that anybody knew about. If he did, they had given up on him long ago. Smokey seemed to have lived a largely unremarkable life. In fact, he probably hadn't been given as much attention in the entire time he was alive as he was about to get now. One thing bound to get a great deal of attention was that the dinginess of Smokey's Court Street room was miles from this pristine spot above the Burrville Falls.

"How do you think he got here?" Palumbo asked, echoing Mike's train of thought.

"I'd bet my pension he didn't walk."

"Staggering was always more his style."

"Exactly," Mike said, sharing the brand of bleak humor that keeps people who see a lot of death from going mad or running off to some less horrific profession.

"It's a fair guess he didn't drive here, either. Did he even know how to drive?"

"As I remember it, he had a license years ago, but we pulled it. I've never seen him in a car since."

"He didn't have a lot of buddies to ride around town with on a Saturday night."

"No." Smokey had been a solitary drinker, a solitary man. "So, how do you think he got here?" Mike repeated Palumbo's question back to him.

"He could have been brought up here and dumped."

Mike gazed back down the incline. "Why would anybody bother to carry him up here?"

Smokey wasn't a big man. He hadn't been particularly hefty to start out with, and, like some drinkers, he had wasted away over the years. Still, this was a considerable haul from the road, no matter how slight the body you were hauling, and dead weight was notoriously difficult to maneuver. In addition, there had been no attempt to conceal him in the woods just beyond here.

"Why all the way up here?" Mike asked again, mostly of himself.

"Maybe somebody's got a thing for riverbanks," Palumbo said. "What do you think there could be about riverbanks that turns this guy on?"

"Beats me."

"This could be a pattern, or it might mean nothing at all," said a voice Mike recognized but didn't register immediately because it didn't belong here. "It could simply be a coincidence."

Caroline wasn't looking at Mike when he turned toward her. She was gazing down at the body the same way Mike and Palumbo had been until her comment interrupted their observations. Now both detectives were staring at her instead, as if she were just as incongruous to this lovely site as the stiff, cold body on the ground.

"Lady, you aren't supposed to be here," Palumbo began.

"She's a friend of mine," Mike said. "Excuse us a minute. I'll be right back."

Mike took Caroline's elbow and steered her away toward the trees. "What are you doing here?" he asked.

"You said I could come. Back at Willow's house. Remember?"

Mike vaguely recalled Caroline asking him about where he was going, but he couldn't honestly say he remembered agreeing that she should come along.

"This could be a major crime scene," he said. "You're a civilian. You shouldn't be here."

"I'm also a professional. My center has occasionally been called in to consult on cases like this one. If this really is a pattern killing, that is."

"What center are you talking about?"

"I'm co-owner of a psychological counseling center," Caroline answered, sounding as cool as he did skeptical. "Police often consult psychologists in the case of pattern killings, seeking a psychological profile of the murderer."

"We haven't yet determined that this is a murder."

"I'd say you're fairly close to doing just that, aren't you?"

Mike stared down at her for a moment. "Look, Caro, I really can't talk right now." He took her elbow again and began walking toward the incline, urging her along in front of him. "How about getting together later?"

"I can see you're busy," she said, pulling her elbow away. She looked up at him with a smile that could hardly have been less sincere. "Unfortunately, I think I'm going to be just as busy later."

Before he could answer, she was off down the embankment, keeping her back admirably straight considering that she had to scurry along to keep from stumbling on the incline.

Dammit, Mike grumbled to himself. He hadn't handled that very well. But then, he never seemed to handle anything very well around her. Open mouth, insert foot was S.O.P. when it came to anything concerning Caro Hardin.

He watched her traverse the slope and head along the path to the cider mill. Dappled sunlight caught the reddish glints in her hair, and Mike felt each one like a spark in his heart.

CAROLINE'S ANGER seethed inside her as she pulled her car onto the high-crowned road so fast that gravel spit from beneath her wheels. She knew exactly where this reaction came from, but that didn't make her any less angry. Folks in northern New York only—being treated like she wasn't a person to be taken seriously.

That was what Mike had just done, and coming from him the insult was even more bitter to swallow. Who did he think he was anyway? What gave him the right to take her by the elbow and usher her out of the yard where the big boys were playing, as if she were some freckle-faced tomboy who had stuck her nose in where she wasn't wanted.

It had taken only moments for Caroline's fury to propel her over the quarter mile to the house where she had last seen Willow. She whipped the steering wheel to the right, and the car squealed into the driveway with yet another spray of gravel. She tromped on the brake so hard that she was thrown against her seat belt as the car jolted to a stop just short of the slope that led to the barn at the back of the property. She had been only partly conscious of driving here. She had probably done so for no better reason than that she knew this place and it was close to the scene of the outrage at the falls—and she wasn't referring to whatever might have happened to the old guy who lay dead up there.

That thought calmed her down some. She certainly shouldn't be acting as if what had happened to her was anywhere near as terrible as what had happened to him. She could still see his face and the stubble of unshaven beard in white and gray patches on his chin. He had looked so small there on the ground, as if he weren't a full-grown man at all but a boy whom life had aged and worn before his time.

Why would anybody feel it necessary to kill such a man?

She had seen no weapon with which he might have threatened someone. And the defeated softness in his face, the way his small hands were curled nearly closed, all but hiding his chipped and blackened fingernails, told her this man had not been the aggressor in whatever had befallen him last night.

Of course, that was an instinctive judgment on her part, and hadn't Mike recently told her that judgments should be based on fact? The reminder of him aroused her anger once more, but she couldn't seem to get him out of her head for long. Where did he, a small-town cop, get the nerve to turn down what was practically an offer of professional expertise in a tough case?

Wait. Who was she kidding? The truth was that her partner, Helena, was the one who had been called in by the Westchester police in a couple of murder investigations when they hadn't a clue to the killer. Caroline had sat in on those consultations and listened avidly and coordinated public relations for the center. She and Helena had discussed the cases in depth, as they often did, and her partner had complimented Caroline on offering some important insights of her own. But she certainly wasn't the expert.

Still, Mike Schaeffer didn't know that, and he had behaved as if her credentials meant nothing. How dare he do that? She was, after all, a paraprofessional at the center already and on her way to her desired degree. And she still knew a lot more about human nature, especially the mixed-up kind, than probably his whole police force put together did. She might very well have been able to help him find his damned killer. Instead, he had given her some party line and hustled her out of the way.

As Caroline's thoughts ran in that familiar, bitter circle, she got out of the car and slammed the door behind her. She was too worked up to sit still.

And she was definitely too worked up to deal with the fact that Mike Schaeffer's car was just now pulling off the road and into the driveway only yards from where she stood, wishing she had never come back to this town.

Chapter Eight

Caroline had used the phrase "last person in the world I want to see" before, but she had never meant it as deeply and completely as she did right now. Mike Schaeffer pulled to a stop in his sedan that was so drab you could guess it was a police car because no one else would buy anything so unattractive. She watched the car door open as it occurred to her that if she could will him back up the hill and out of her sight she would do exactly that. The guy was driving her crazy!

She was still fuming, and his cautious smile as he approached told her that he knew it.

"Hi. How're you doing?" he asked.

That infuriated her even more. How like a man to act a little sheepish in order to get around a woman after he had done some pigheaded guy thing to make her angry in the first place. That tactic certainly wasn't going to work with her.

"I was doing just fine until you arrived."

"I followed you up here to apologize. I didn't mean to be so abrupt back there."

"You won't get any argument from me about that."

He studied her for a moment before answering, "I didn't expect that I would. But I had hoped you'd give me a chance to explain and to make you an offer."

"What kind of offer?"

"First the explanation." He stepped toward her, closer than she wanted. "You see, I get very caught up in things when I'm working. I tend to think only about the problem I'm dealing with. Consequently, that isn't a good time to interrupt me. I can't handle having my train of thought derailed. Doesn't that ever happen to you?"

"Yes, I suppose it does." Caroline still wasn't very inclined to give him so much as an inch right now, but he did have a point. She did understand what he meant about getting so absorbed in work that you become oblivious to everything and everybody else.

"Anyway, I was rude, and I apologize. The last thing I want to do is make you angry with me."

His serious gray eyes were suddenly looking intently into hers. They held her for an instant, and in that moment she knew she would probably forgive this man anything.

What a dangerous notion! Still, he had explained himself, and he certainly did sound sincere.

"What was that offer you mentioned?" she asked, relenting a bit on her indignant stance.

"I'd like you to work with me on these homicides."

She was taken aback. That was just about the last thing she had expected him to say, and for once she didn't have a response at the ready.

"You said you had been involved in several investigations, doing psychological profiling, that kind of thing."

"I thought you said you weren't ready to classify these deaths as murders," she countered.

"That's our official position for the moment, but it's not going to hold up for long. I'm sure you know what's going to happen when the press get their hands on this."

"Well, two cases doesn't exactly a serial killer make," Caroline pointed out.

"Technically, you're right about that. The FBI requires half a dozen bodies before they'll call it a serial case. Unfortunately, the papers won't make such fine distinctions. This is too hot a story for them to pass up, especially when the Syracuse reporters get wind of what's going on up here."

Syracuse was about twenty-five miles south of Watertown and the closest thing there was to a big city in this vicinity. And Mike was right. The press would have a field day with this sort of stuff, and the result would be a lot of public panic and pressure to find the killer.

"So, what's the verdict, Caroline? Will you help me out?"

She gazed back at him and sighed. Should she even consider taking on a task she wasn't sure she'd be equal to, risking making a fool of herself.

"I'm not asking you to do this just for me," he went on. "Maybe you could think about doing it for your hometown."

She almost laughed at that one. "That isn't really the issue for me," she replied carefully.

"Then what is the issue?"

"Don't you have a local psychologist or psychiatrist who could handle this?"

"Not really. The two here in town are strictly small-time counselors, focusing mainly on marriage-and-career stuff."

"I'm not exactly a licensed expert on abnormal psychology myself, you know." She went on to explain the current state of her credentials and how she and Helena worked.

"Still," Mike protested, "you've had more hands-on experience than anyone around here. Besides," he added, "I think we could work well together."

"A little while ago you didn't even take me seriously enough to be polite," she pointed out a bit acerbically.

"That will never happen again. I give you my word."

He moved closer still and took hold of her shoulders.

"Please, Caro," he said. "I may need you."

Again she was aware of the difficulty of denying this man. And it made her worry about maintaining her all-important professional stance. After all, the feeling of having Mike's hands on her seemed out of line for a purely business relationship. Still, somehow none of that seemed as important right now as his admission of needing her.

"All right. I'll do what I can to help."

"That's wonderful!" His face lit up.

"I hope so," Caroline said, stepping out of his grasp and attempting a more formal tone.

"Of course, the department will pay you," Mike was saying. "We may not be able to manage as much as you're used to at your center, but I'm sure we can come up with a respectable fee."

"A fee?" It was one thing to lend a helping hand and another to take money for it. "I'd prefer to volunteer my services," she said. "As you put it earlier, for my hometown."

She flashed him what she hoped was a charitable smile and began walking toward her car before he could object.

"Are you headed back to the hotel?" he asked.

"Well, I'm not sure." What were her plans, anyway? Everything seemed to have flown out of her head as soon as Mike Schaeffer had shown up.

"By the way, how did you happen to stop at this place?" Mike asked, indicating the house.

Caroline stared at him as the significance of that question sunk in. She hadn't told him about leaving Willow here because of what he might think. And she still didn't want him to think those things.

"A friend of mine lives here," she improvised.

"Is that right?" Mike's tone suddenly changed. He sounded almost angry. "How do you know Nate Conklin?"

She had to be careful. Mike was sharp. One wrong word and he'd figure out that she didn't know this Nate Conklin guy at all.

"Did Willow introduce you? That's what I thought. She's always been pretty impressed by him. Most women are. He's a real man of the world, too, so I suppose he gets down your way quite often."

Caroline didn't comment. She observed the dark shadows deepening in Mike's eyes and across his face. He was truly upset, and she wasn't sure why. She almost might have said he was jealous, but she didn't want to jump to conclusions. Instead, she contented herself with being grateful that his agitation would most likely keep him from examining her acquaintance with Conklin too shrewdly.

"I'm not surprised that you were charmed by him, too," Mike said. "Why should you be any different from all the other women who think he's so wonderful?"

"I take it you don't like Mr. Conklin much."

"Not true," Mike said. "I like him just fine."

"He charmed you, too, I guess."

"Not really. He's simply a good guy. Charm's got nothing to do with it. I said that to make him sound like some slick phoney you shouldn't trust, but that couldn't be farther from the truth. I don't blame you for being *friends* with him."

He was jealous, all right. His emphasis on the word "friends" told Caroline that.

Something else told her it was also time to take her chances with the truth.

"We aren't friends," she said quietly, poking her toe at a particularly large, green leaf that had fallen onto the path from an overhanging branch. "I only said that to put you off the track. I don't even know Nate Conklin, and I apologize for telling you I did."

Mike studied her for a moment before asking, "Then what are you doing at his house?"

Caroline sighed. Maybe it would be for the best for Mike to know the whole truth.

"I was here the other day looking for Willow, and when I left the cider mill just now, this was the closest place I knew of to blow off steam."

"Why would you look for Willow here?"

Caroline turned away from her car and began walking slowly toward Nate Conklin's back porch, kicking at loose gravel along the path. Mike kept pace with her, obviously not wanting to miss a word of her answer.

"Because this is where I dropped her off the night I last saw her."

"Was Nate here when you dropped her off?" asked Mike, looking up at the house, which still appeared as deserted as when Caroline was last here.

"The house was dark. I don't think there was anyone here."

"What was Willow's excuse for coming here?"

Caroline heard the skepticism in his tone. "Her reason for coming here was to get away from her husband. She said this was a friend's place, and that she had permission to be here." Caroline didn't mention her growing suspicion that Willow had actually made her entrance through a window, rather than as a invited guest.

"Didn't you think it strange that a married woman should choose a bachelor's house as a hideout?"

They had reached the porch steps. Caroline turned to confront Mike. "A moment ago you agreed that from now on you were going to take me seriously as a professional. Right?"

"Right," Mike answered, looking puzzled at the change of subject.

"Then that means trusting my judgment. In my judgment, Willow was sincerely afraid for her safety the night I left her here, and it was Justin she was afraid of."

"All right. I'll trust your judgment, but I need an agreement from you, too."

Caroline was suddenly wary. Mike was proving to have an unpredictable effect on her. "What agreement is that?" she asked.

"If we are going to work together on these homicides, I want to know that you will be more honest with me than you have been about Willow."

"Agreed," she said.

"Good."

"One more thing." She took his arm to stop him as he was about to walk back toward the cars. "If I am going to work with you to find your murderer, you'll have to work with me to find Willow."

He hesitated a moment before answering, "Agreed."

"Then the first thing we have to do is search this house. Which, by the way, I didn't know was a bachelor's house the night I dropped Willow off." She began tugging him up the steps to the porch.

"Wait a minute. I already followed you into one house without permission today. That is called illegal entry. I'm not about to do it again."

"But we have probable cause," she answered in her most convincing tone.

"Probable cause of what?"

"That there could be evidence inside relating to the whereabouts of a missing person."

"Caro, that's ridicu—" To his credit he stopped himself at her glare. "We still don't have a warrant," he amended.

"Well, warrant or not, *I'm* going in. So arrest me if you want."

Caroline walked resolutely across the porch to the window and pushed it up.

"How did you know that window was open?"

There was that skepticism again, and she really couldn't blame him.

"I found it the other day," she said.

He grabbed her arm as she was about to climb through. "Did you also go inside the other day?"

"Yes, I did," she said, uncomfortable that he had caught her in another sin of omission.

"So I assume you searched the place already. Did you find anything?"

"No, but I didn't take the time to look around thoroughly."

"Why not?"

"Because it made me nervous to be in there by myself," she said with some exasperation.

Mike dropped her arm. "You should be nervous about sneaking into somebody's house when you haven't been invited. It's against the law."

"I said I was nervous because I was alone. But you're here this time." Caroline didn't wait for him to answer that. She was through the window before he could stop her. "Would you feel more comfortable if I unlocked the door and invited you in?"

If Mike found that amusing, he didn't bother to laugh. He climbed through the window after her.

"I've given this some thought," she said, ignoring how obviously displeased he was to be here. "I know exactly where we should start our search."

"Why am I not surprised by that?"

Caroline ignored his sarcasm and glanced around. Everything looked exactly as it had the last time she was here. She would guess that no one else had been in the house since then. She headed for the stairway to the second floor.

"There are two bedrooms upstairs," she said. "One of them is obviously a man's. The other must be a guest room. Willow probably slept there. I want to give that room a more careful going-over than I did the other day."

If Mike had an contradictory theory about which bedroom Willow might have slept in, he kept it to himself. After some hesitation and a loud sigh, he followed Caroline up the stairs and into the guest bedroom.

Their first examination was discouraging. They didn't find a thing to indicate that Willow or anybody else had been here recently. "I think I'll check the next room," Mike said.

Caroline didn't comment on the fact that the next room was Nate Conklin's. With Mike out of sight, she began searching more thoroughly than she had before. The first thing she did was pull the bedclothes down and feel around under the pillows and between the sheets, but she found nothing. She was about to remake the bed and turn her attention to the closet when she noticed that the corner of the mattress nearest the pillow was slightly elevated. She slid her hand under the mattress, and, sure enough her fingers hit something.

It felt like a book. It turned out to be an expensive diary, with a fabric cover and smooth, thick pages. Caroline instantly remembered that Willow had brought such a notebook with her on her few visits to Westchester. A quick glance at the pages indicated that it was indeed her journal.

"Look what I found!" Caroline called out enthusiastically as she hurried next door to show Mike the journal.

"What is it?" he asked as he took the rose-colored volume from her hand.

"Willow's journal. She always brought one with her when she came to visit me. She said she needed at least one place where she could be alone with her private thoughts." Caroline looked around at the simple house with its dark wood furnishings and clean white walls. "Maybe she felt the same way here."

Mike made an absentminded sound in response. He was busy skimming the pages of Willow's journal.

"Mike." Caroline grasped his arm. "I don't think we should be reading her private journal. The point is that this is a very special possession of Willow's. I don't think she would take everything else she owned and leave this behind—at least not voluntarily."

That made him look up. "What are you getting at?" he asked.

"There are a number of possibilities. She could have left this behind deliberately as a signal—maybe to me—that something was wrong. Or she could have left it behind because she was going somewhere with someone she was afraid to have read it. Or..." Caroline hesitated, because this last thought was the most sinister, and she didn't like saying it out loud.

"Or what?"

"Or the journal didn't get packed with her things because Willow didn't do that packing. Somebody else packed for her, and they didn't know about the journal under the mattress."

"You mean they packed for her against her will." ·

"Yes. That's what I mean." Admitting it sent a shiver of apprehension straight up Caroline's spine.

"Good deducing, Caro. You're starting to think like a detective." Mike smiled approvingly, and the effect on his rugged features was most appealing.

"Or like a psychologist," Caroline said, feeling quite flattered.

"I think I prefer the alternative where Willow leaves the journal here because she's afraid of having somebody else read it. Her husband, for example. That's how I'd feel if I were a married woman who had written this."

"What did you find in there?" Caroline grabbed the journal from him and began leafing through it.

"I haven't time for a thorough reading, but she does mention a number of men in some interesting scenarios," he said wryly.

"Where do you see that?"

"You'll get to it. When you do, I think you will have to agree that this supports Justin's claims about Willow's, shall we call them, indiscretions?"

Caroline didn't answer. She was skimming journal pages. Mike was right about the number of men's names, but as Caroline stopped to read through a couple of entries, she couldn't agree with Mike's conclusion.

"She doesn't write about these things as if they actually happened. She writes as if she *wishes* they would happen."

"I'm not sure I see that there's much difference," Mike said with his usual skepticism. "She's a married woman writing about men other than her husband."

"There's all the difference in the world, Mike. These are fantasies, nothing more. They are very likely her substitute for actually acting in the unfaithful manner she has been accused of."

"Is that your conclusion as a professional?"

Caroline studied his face. Was he being sarcastic? She couldn't tell.

"Yes, that is my professional opinion. Besides," Caroline said, "there is the obvious fact that she left it here to take into account. What explanation do you have for that? Especially if your theory were right, and Willow was using the journal as a confessor to her indiscretions. Wouldn't that make her even less likely to leave it behind?"

"I admit that is puzzling, but there could be a reason for it. She could have forgotten it. Or maybe she left with Nate or some other man, and she didn't want him to read about her extracurricular activities. She hid it and plans to retrieve it when she returns. That sounds like a more believable scenario to me."

"I don't think so."

"Don't tell me why. Let me guess. Your instincts say that she's in trouble and that you shouldn't believe her husband or her housekeeper or even the evidence of this book."

"Something like that, but more concrete. I believe Willow."

"Well, what is concrete to *me* is that I have two probable homicides to investigate and I can't really afford the time to get into what is most likely a purely domestic situation—a case of a wife taking a voluntary sabbatical from her husband with another man."

Despite his promise to help her, which he would doubtless honor, Caroline could see that he had made up his mind that whatever time he spent investigating Willow's disappearance would be time wasted. "It seems we will have to agree to disagree on this for the time being."

"Good. Then we can get on to the killings? But first let me do one more thing that could convince you I'm right about this. I want to take you to talk with Justin himself."

Caroline had been toying with that idea herself. She would like to put some questions directly to the man in question. She might be able to tell something from what he had to say—or what he didn't have to say.

"Let's go," she said.

JUSTIN'S OFFICES seemed to suit him perfectly. He had taken over one of the old Victorian houses on Washington Street, restored the exterior, gingerbread and all, and converted the interior to something that looked more California than north country.

Great care had been taken to make his personal office look like anything but an office. There was a desk, but it was small and delicate and off to the side, where it would be less conspicuous than the room's focal point: a conversational grouping of chairs, couches and occasional tables. Each piece was lovely and blended well with the others, creating an air of informality out of exacting detail. The result was probably precisely what Justin had aimed for: utter charm.

Of course, Willow had raised some doubts about Justin Fowler's brand of charm. Consequently, when the man came hurrying in to greet them enthusiastically, for the first time in their brief and superficial acquaintance, Caroline observed him with a deliberately critical eye.

"What can I get you?" he asked. "Sparkling water? Fruit juice? Herb tea?"

He certainly was right up to the minute in the health food arena, Caroline thought as she politely refused. Was he New Age prone in any other way, she wondered. He hardly fit the laid-back, West Coast mold in either appearance or demeanor. His suit was recognizably pricey and a fine choice for his trim, compact frame. He was nearly bald on top, though the hair at the sides didn't betray a hint of graying. But when he smoothed one side with a diamond-ringed hand, Caroline had to squelch the knee-jerk reaction of associating him with mobster dons.

The association did, however, provide a perfect adjective for Justin. He was slick. The way men of power are often slick. The way Don Juans are often slick. The way some noted sociopaths have been slick.

Caroline told herself that that last thought was hardly warranted by what she had observed of Justin thus far and that she must do her best to remain objective. Yet one thing she did know about such extremely polished people was that they had to work very hard to get that way—which always made her wonder what was underneath, motivating them to take such pains with the surface.

Chapter Nine

"You know how some women are," Justin said, looking mainly at Mike.

"No, I don't. Please, tell me," Caroline answered, not wanting to give Mike a chance to say something she might dislike him for.

"Let's put it this way," Justin said. "Willow has her...spiteful side."

"Could you be more specific about that?"

"She likes to...taunt me now and then. And she's not above making me look bad in front of other people."

"That must be very hard on you," Caroline said, trying to sound like a commiserating friend. Meanwhile, the orange juice she had reluctantly accepted, then taken only one sip of had turned to a sour taste in the back of her mouth.

"I have more than once been humiliated by her making a public spectacle of herself." Justin assumed a long-suffering look.

"There must be a lot of talk around town about that kind of thing."

Justin stared at Caroline. "Actually, most people are kind and want to spare my feelings, so they don't say much."

"That certainly has always been my experience of how Watertonians behave." Caroline pretended not to notice the nudge Mike gave her when she said that.

A half hour later, after they had left Justin's office, Mike nudged her again. "What was that all about back there?"

"What was what all about?"

"Why were you so sarcastic with him?"

They were walking down a narrow brick pathway bordered by immaculate flower beds. Everything in Justin Fowler's world was so deliberately and totally correct. How would he feel about a wife who turned out not to fit that exacting standard? What might he do in response?

"Don't stall me," Mike said, nudging her a third time. "You know what I'm talking about."

"Sure I do, and I'm not stalling. I was thinking."

"About what?"

"About how the Willow Gilchrist Fowler he was describing isn't the same woman I have known for over fifteen years."

They had reached the parking lot and were strolling toward Mike's unmarked patrol car, having dropped hers back at the hotel. "Maybe you only think you know her so well. Maybe she's changed since you two were close," he said. "Do you understand what I mean?"

"I understand." Caroline stopped by the passenger side of the car. "I also understand that Justin could be lying."

"Why would he do that?"

"To make us think that he's the victim in this situation."

"What situation?" Mike sounded as if his patience might be running short. "Can't you see that you're probably imagining that Willow is in danger when she's really not?"

Caroline didn't see that at all. What she did see, when she happened to look up, was Justin standing at a window on the second floor of his office building. An instant later she wasn't so sure because Justin lifted his hand for a friendly wave. Still, Caroline was glad that Mike had driven her here. She'd had enough of panic in the past few days to last her for quite some time. With Mike she would be safe, even if Justin and his cold eyes were on her trail.

She let Mike open the car door and take her hand as she stepped inside. She wanted Justin to see that protective gesture and know that, unlike Willow, Caroline was not alone and vulnerable.

ONCE BACK at her hotel, Caroline was feeling vulnerable precisely because she was not alone. Mike had walked her to her room, though she had insisted that was not necessary. He had taken the key card from her hand and used it to open her door. He had stepped inside only as far as the entryway, and she had felt reasonably secure up to that point. Then he closed the door behind him, and all delusions of safety disappeared.

He backed himself against the door and pulled her to him.

"Mike, don't..." she said, but the words were too late and too feeble to halt the inevitable.

He crushed her against him so close she could barely move and covered her mouth with his own before she could say more. He kissed her hard like that for a long moment, then she felt his tongue touch hers. He tasted good, and his lips were warm. In fact, she felt heat all along his body, spreading into hers. It had been cool outside, but only seconds in his arms had banished any memory of a chill.

She had fantasized this kiss more times than she had kept track of over the years, but those fantasies had been of a teenaged girl kissing a young man. That was hardly who she and Mike were now. She was a healthy, sensual woman. He was a powerfully attractive man. Whatever happened between them tonight would not be kid's stuff.

As if he might also have come to the same realization, Mike's tongue began to probe. What had been warmth was suddenly hot and demanding, stroking in and in and in again and again, as if he intended to pierce any and all obstacles that kept him from the very core of her.

She thought of struggling away from him, but suddenly she wasn't certain why. She didn't really want him to stop. This was too sweet. This was too fiercely blazing. This was too much of everything she had always longed for with a man to have it stop. Yet she was afraid, but with a fear like none she had ever known. Instead of warning her away, it inflamed her more. This was dangerous, yet that danger was thrilling. Her intended struggle turned sinuous instead as she ground her body hungrily against his.

She had worn a jacket and a cotton sweater to ward off the chilly weather. His hand was beneath them both before she even felt him move. His fingers probed her flesh as insistently as his tongue was marauding her mouth, but his need was no greater than her own.

She reached between them and grasped the hand closing over the fullness of her breast. She closed her fingers over his as he squeezed her, kneaded her, her nipples throbbing beneath the assault.

They were both moaning now, making hoarse, inarticulate throaty sounds. They had sagged against the door, her pressing into him, him gripping her hips to force their bodies together as close as the clothing between them would allow.

They began the slide downward together to the rough carpet of the entryway. She let him roll her over till he was on top of her. She would have let him do anything he wished.

She even helped him pull her skirt above her hips and settle his body between her thighs. He began moving against her, the hard bulge in his jeans. The denim tortured the silk of her panties, and she could feel her wetness there. She wished he could feel it, too.

Her hand was still over his at her breast. She guided him downward, between their undulating bodies, as she answered his movements with her own. She felt him tense all over as he touched the wet heat of her. She did not need to guide him further. He slipped his fingers beneath the lace and stroked those lips for a moment, then plunged inside of her and matched the rhythm of his thrusts to that of his hips pounding against her.

Caroline tried to keep moving as well, but suddenly she could not. She went limp and still, as if paralyzed by what he was making her feel. Her mind was a blank except for the thought that she wanted more and more of him, forever. Then the shudder began. It started in her loins and beneath her stomach, then moved downward to capture his fingers in a clutch of desire that pulsated with each thrust he made into her.

The cataclysm was so intense that she thought it might shake her apart. Her hips lifted beneath him. His mouth only partly stopped the cry that rose from her throat. She hung there in that shuddering, ecstatic oblivion for endless moments. Then she was still, with the most wonderfully languid warmth she had ever known spreading through her body like molten peace.

MIKE LOOKED DOWN at the woman in his arms. After a mind-boggling orgasm, she had fallen asleep, her dark hair caught in damp strands along the borders of her face like a dusky frame for her beauty. Passion had painted her cheeks a deep pink, and a dewiness softened her face, making him half expect to find tiny droplets at the tips of the long lashes that hid huge brown eyes. She was asleep, but she could hardly have looked more vital and alive.

Mike moved silently to touch the damp strands at her cheek and, with a feather-soft gesture, ease them back from her skin and smoothed them off her face. His fingers hovered over her lips for a moment, then he pulled his hand away without disturbing her slumber.

Her skirt was completely rumpled, and Mike pulled the polished cotton back down over her long, shapely legs, smoothing out the wrinkles along the way. All the while he held her in the curve of his arm, perfectly still and protected like a chick beneath a sheltering wing.

Nonetheless, she began to stir, stretching in a long, sinuous movement that made him gasp at her unconscious sensuousness. Her eyes opened slowly, blinking twice before glancing around with some surprise. They were still on the floor of the entryway to her room. She looked up at him, and recognition filled her gaze.

In seconds the flush that had been only in her cheeks spread down her neck. She sat up quickly, smoothing her skirt. There was no mistaking her embarrassment and confusion. She struggled to stand. Mike took her arm to help, but she pulled away and scrambled to her feet on her own.

"You have to go now," she said, her voice quavering. She cleared her throat. "You really must leave right now," she repeated more insistently this time.

Mike had pulled himself to his feet after her. He stood staring down at her, and she stepped aside quietly as if to widen the gulf between them.

"There's nothing wrong with what happened between us here," he said quietly.

"I—don't want to talk about it," she said with surprising vehemence. "I just...I want you out of here."

"All right." He stepped toward the door. "But I still think—"

"Please..." she interrupted.

Mike sighed. "I'm sorry you feel that way." He opened the door and was about to leave. "I hope we will still be able to work together."

Caroline stared at him, as if she might have forgotten all about that aspect of their relationship. "Of course, we can work together," she said, with obviously deliberate composure. "That is another matter entirely."

"I'm glad to hear that," said Mike, but as he closed the door behind him he could hardly have been farther from feeling glad about anything.

AFTER LEAVING Caroline, Mike took his car back to the police station.

"We've been trying to get you for almost an hour now," said the officer on desk duty. "Isn't your beeper working?"

Mike patted the side of his belt, but nothing was there. "I must have left it in the car."

The officer regarded Mike with a curious expression. "You were walking around without your beeper? I'd have thought a guy like you would wear that thing into the shower."

Mike smiled. "Call it a momentary lapse. Everybody's guilty of one of those now and then."

"If you say so." The officer sounded skeptical. "Anyway, we've got what looks like it could be a break in the riverbank murders."

"What kind of a break?" Mike's smile had disappeared. He was all business now and dead serious about it.

"There's Palumbo." The officer gestured toward the stocky figure just coming in.

"Earlier this evening, we got a report on something real interesting," Palumbo said almost before he was in the door.

"What's that?"

"Let's go into your office and get comfortable."

Mike nodded. Palumbo had a reputation for milking the suspense of a situation whenever he could. Mike was short on patience for that kind of thing right now, but he headed for his office anyway. Palumbo winked at the desk officer and followed Mike inside.

"This guy called. Says he's got a cleaning contract for a building over on Stone Street, the one right behind the Carriage House. Know which place I mean?"

"Yeah, yeah, I know. Get on with it." Mike was sitting in his desk chair running the zipper of his windbreaker up and down in an increasingly agitated motion.

"Seems he's been stripping floors in there this week, and tonight he comes upon something that upsets him." Palumbo was watching Mike and the zipper. Palumbo might have been planning to drag the story out some more, but he plunged straight on instead. "He rolls up the rug in one of the offices and finds a big, dark red stain underneath. Says it looks like blood. So I went over there. Sure enough. It's blood all right."

"How long ago was that?"

"Two, three hours."

"Why didn't you call me?" Mike had stopped working the zipper, but he didn't look any less agitated.

"I figured it wasn't enough to go on to get you in here from wherever you might be, especially since I saw you heading off Burrville Road this afternoon hot on the trail of that woman." Palumbo eyed Mike with smile. "So I used my discretion."

"Okay, okay. I get the message," Mike said. "So get on with your story before I grow roots in this chair."

"Well, the cleaning guy says it looks to his professional eye like somebody washed out that old rug and might have thought they got all the blood out, not realizing they couldn't likely do that. Then, as the rug sat there, what was left in it seeped onto the floor, and that's what he found there tonight."

"So? What's this got to do with the riverbank homicides?"

"The cleaning guy says it hasn't been there too long. It's fairly fresh. That gave me a hunch. So I took a couple of patches from the carpet, and I sent them to the lab for a fast check. And guess what."

"What?"

"That blood came from the first vic, the John Doe we found down by Black River." Palumbo grinned with the air of an actor who has just given a fine performance.

"Are you absolutely certain about that?" Mike asked.

"Absolutely."

"You should have gotten in touch with me the minute you found that out."

"I tried." Palumbo threw his arms up in a gesture of exasperation. "I couldn't raise you anywhere."

Mike shuffled his feet under the desk and sat up straighter. "Okay, you tried. So, what happened next?"

"I went over to the building in question and started nosing around. There were still a couple of offices open, and you know how I can charm those secretaries." Palumbo flashed a smile that showed perfect white teeth.

"Yeah, I know. You're the Italian stallion." Mike laughed for the first time in hours.

"Well, what I find out over there is that the office in question is vacant—no rental agreement with anyone—but they got a night watchman named Lester Pickett. Does that ring a bell with you?"

"I'm not sure."

"It rang a bell with me. I've run old Lester in a couple of times."

"On what charges?"

"Drunk and disorderly. I'd call it more like chronic ornery disposition and a taste for beating up on people."

"That's exactly what I'm saying. Hair-trigger temper type. Somebody gets him riled, and he pops off."

"Were any of the incidents serious?" Mike asked.

"He got drunk and beat a guy up really bad once. Put him in the hospital for a couple of weeks."

"Have you got an address?"

Palumbo nodded and smiled that charming smile again. "I thought you'd never ask."

LESTER PICKETT lived on a part of Leray Street that might have seen better days, but not recently. The paint was long gone from the address, and the porch had sagged a foot or so at the corner where the splintered steps led to the door. Palumbo had already checked and found out it was Lester's night off as a security guard.

Mike's first knock brought no response. Palumbo was standing off to the side, out of range of the door window with its rag of dingy curtain. He didn't actually have his gun out, but the corner of his sport coat was flipped back, and his hand was nearby.

"Is there anybody home?" Mike called out.

Then they heard what sounded like movement inside and low, urgent voices. Palumbo backed himself against the wall and put his hand on his gun.

"What you want?" came an unfriendly sounding voice from the other side of the door.

"Police," Mike said. "We need to talk to Lester Pickett. We understand he lives here."

No response.

"You'd better send Lester out here or tell us where we can find him. Otherwise, he's going to be in big trouble," called Mike.

The silence inside continued for a moment. Then the door began to open, and a very skinny man edged his way, very cautiously, through the opening and onto the porch.

"I'm Lester Pickett," he said. "What do you want?"

LATER THAT NIGHT Mike had called Caroline from the station house to ask her if she was still willing to work with the police department on the murders. When she answered a definite though wary yes, he had said he'd get her copies of the most pertinent information from the files on both cases and suggested they meet for breakfast the next morning. Fortunately, he had not brought the material himself. She hadn't been ready to see him in person.

She could hardly believe what she had allowed to happen between them that afternoon. What had she been thinking of? The answer to that was, she hadn't been thinking at all. Her body had taken over from her brain in a way that was not only unusual for her but disturbing, as well. She couldn't be stupid enough to imagine that this was anything more than the acting out of an adolescent fantasy, could she? Yet she could feel herself teetering on the brink of making a total fool of herself, and she wasn't about to let herself fall over the edge.

Was Mike feeling regrets, too? That could explain why he had dispatched a patrolman to deliver the dark pink accordian file to her room rather than coming himself. She told herself she was glad he had. She didn't want to think about what might have happened if Mike had shown up at her door. Her fantasies of Mike Schaeffer had her in enough trouble already.

Caroline kept herself preoccupied by studying the contents of the file long into the night. She learned that they had a strong suspect now, a night watchman named Lester Pickett. According to notes dated that same day, Detective Joseph Palumbo considered Pickett a viable candidate. Mike's notes didn't indicate the same enthusiasm for that theory, which would explain why he still wanted Caroline on the case. He wanted her to come up with a profile of the killer if she could. He then could check out this suspect and any others against that profile. In other words, her hunch was that *his* hunch was that Pickett was not their man, and Mike needed corroboration of that.

At first, Caroline had been unnerved by what she had agreed to do. She had thought about calling her partner, Helena, but decided to put that off until she really needed her expertise.

Instead, she had studied and pondered and made lots of notes. That process had gone a long way to stilling her fears of inadequacy.

So why, the next morning, did she feel so nervous as she prepared to meet Mike for their breakfast conference?

She knew the answer to that question, and there was no point in pretending she didn't. She might be ready to tackle these murder cases—one of the most challenging assignments of her career thus far—but she was not even close to ready to see Mike face-to-face again. The top of her bed attested to that fact. It was heaped with every single piece of clothing she had brought with her on this trip. She had been trying on various outfits for almost an hour now without coming up with one that would make her feel both confident and at ease in this encounter.

The truth of the matter was that wardrobe wasn't the key—unless she could dig up a suit of armor for her emotions as well as her body. After their last shocking meeting, she was going to feel vulnerable with Mike, and there was nothing she could do to prevent that.

Finally, out of desperation to put something on, she chose a drapy mauve suit with a cream-colored shell. The effect was softer than she would have preferred, but since this wasn't meant to be a business trip, she had left all her more tailored clothes back home.

When she walked into the hotel dining room, she saw that Mike had chosen a corner table where they could talk privately. As she approached, she attempted her most businesslike smile and willed it to stay put on her face.

He looked different from the other times she had seen him, she noted. He was wearing a suit. It was nicely tailored, its squared shoulders complementing the breadth of his chest most attractively, and the subtle fitting at the waist doing the same for his trimness. He was even wearing a tie.

Maybe Mike didn't need somebody to pick out his clothes for him after all. Maybe all he needed was a reason to care about what he put on. Might he think of her in those terms?

"Good morning," he said, reaching out to take her hand. "You look lovely today."

She had no choice but to take his hand, at least for a single businesslike instant. Unfortunately, she had overestimated her capacity to be equal to any physical contact with him at all. The moment their fingers touched she imagined his hands touching her everywhere and swirling her emotions into the worst turmoil she had ever known.

A flush stole up her throat, and she felt the heat sear her cheeks. She struggled to regain her composure, more certain than ever of the potency and the danger of this fantasy she couldn't seem to shake herself free of. She needed desperately to get herself under control. She pulled her hand abruptly away from his and sat down before he could move to help her with her chair.

"Let's get right down to business, shall we?" she said briskly. "We have a lot of ground to cover."

Chapter Ten

Caroline tapped the two file folders next to her place setting. "I spent most of the night going over these," she said as she took a spiral notebook and pen from her purse.

"I didn't mean for you to put yourself out," Mike said, sounding truly concerned.

Caroline looked straight at him, willing all personal emotions to desert her. This wasn't a personal thing. They were temporarily working together. She had to establish that right now, and she had to establish it for both of them.

"When I agree to work on a project," she said, "I put everything I have into it. That means thought, energy and time. Sometimes that time doesn't fit into a nine-to-five schedule. I do what needs to be done anyway. I'm sure you can understand that."

She had hoped her words would snap Mike into his all-business mode, but they didn't seem to. His gray eyes were more serious than ever, but they were probing hers. And she herself couldn't help admiring how handsome he looked in his suit, his starched shirt collar making an appealing contrast to his sun-burnished skin. His hair was still a bit overlong, and, today, slicked-back, making him appear just a little dangerous. She felt that danger tingling inside her where her hunger for breakfast should have been.

Mike's voice grated against her sensitized nerves. "I have a reputation for doing what needs to be done myself. Right now, though, I don't think that has anything to do with those files."

Caroline cleared her throat. "If you want us to work together," she said, "I suggest we deal with the business at hand and stay away from whatever personal relationship we may or may not have."

"Which is it, Caro? May or may not?"

His eyes were truly probing now, like a jet of warm light illuminating her most secret places, and she couldn't stop wanting him to take her by the arm and propel her back to her room to finish what they had started there the previous afternoon.

Caroline pushed back her chair. "That attitude answers my question about whether we can work together as professionals." She pushed the file folders toward him. "I don't think so."

Mike caught her wrist. "Don't leave," he said. "I'll behave. I promise."

"Why is it that I don't believe you?"

Mike laughed. "Maybe you know me better than I thought you did."

His laughter and the smile that crinkled the corners of his eyes drew an answering chuckle from Caroline, lightening the moment considerably. She eased her wrist from his grasp and sat back down.

"I really could use your help with these investigations," he said, his gray eyes serious once more.

"I'd like to work on them with you, but the ground rules must be clear from the start."

Mike leaned closer across the table, preempting the direction of her conversation. "I think our killer has some ground rules of his own—the first of which may be that he isn't finished killing yet." He pushed the file folders toward her once more. "You've read these things. What do you think?"

The waitress, who had hung back till now, hurried up to their table as if to take their order before one of them jumped up again.

Mike selected a huge breakfast combination, prompting Caroline to note that his appetite was as manly as the rest of him. Then alarmed at the direction of her thoughts, she gave her hand a mental slap and ordered coffee and a muffin.

"You'll need more fuel than that if you plan to keep up with me," Mike said.

Caroline smiled at the waitress who had been waiting to see if Caroline would change her order as Mike suggested. "Coffee and a muffin will be plenty for now."

"A woman who eats like a bird can be very sexy. It keeps her lean and mean," Mike said with a wink.

"Michael..." Caroline warned, despite her own wayward notion of just moments ago.

He raised his hands in a gesture of surrender. "Sorry. I know, I know. Ground rules."

"I'll bring your coffee," the waitress said quietly.

"So tell me your thoughts on these cases," Mike said after the waitress had bustled away. "Any brainstorms about what we might be dealing with here?"

Caroline took a deep breath and sent up a silent prayer that she would prove as good as she needed to be here.

"First of all," she said, "I'm sure you know the problem with the night watchman, Lester Pickett, as a suspect is that we would have to find some link between him and the second victim, Smokey Rhodes. By the way, do you have a name on the first victim yet?"

"We're working on it."

The waitress filled their coffee cups and placed sugar and cream on the table between them. Caroline waited till the woman left before continuing.

"Of course, that connection could exist, and I assume you're already looking for it," she said.

"We are. We already know that Pickett frequented a number of the same taverns as Rhodes. One bartender even seems to remember them getting into an argument once. This could be a case of Pickett settling old scores."

"It's also possible that Pickett committed the first murder, and the second was done by a copycat," she said.

"Not likely. There are details we didn't release to the media on that first case. The details were still the same with the second case."

"I figured you'd probably done something like that."

The waitress was back with a plate of muffins in one hand and an outsize platter in the other. Mike glanced from her bran and raisins breakfast back to his own hearty meal.

"Go ahead and eat," she told him. "I'm going to be doing most of the talking for a while anyway."

"Sounds good to me." Mike picked up his fork and started on the mound of scrambled eggs in front of him.

Caroline flipped open her spiral notebook. "I'm going to begin with the assumption that we're dealing with a single murderer here. I'm also going to set Lester Pickett aside for a while and continue as if we had no suspects at all and needed a general profile. I will also extrapolate that we have had more than two killings and the others have been essentially the same as these. As we said earlier, two cases don't really make what we would term a pattern in the strictest sense."

"Shoot."

Mike speared a sausage with the gusto of a man who likes to eat, and Caroline couldn't help being reminded of his hearty appetite in other areas, as well. She cleared her throat and quelled the thought.

"Having examined these files, I would say that the first thing we know about this guy is that he may not necessarily be a guy."

Mike's fork hesitated for a moment en route to his mouth.

"Theoretically, a woman could have done these killings, and, at the start, we shouldn't eliminate any possibility. Neither victim was very big in stature, and a strong or hefty woman could have managed the job."

"I hadn't really considered that as a possibility."

"While statistics show that far more men than women commit this kind of crime, I wouldn't want to rule it out entirely."

"You're the expert," said Mike with a smile as he forked up some home fries. "I asked for your opinion. I'm not going to knock holes in it right off the bat.''

''I can give you possible diagnoses,'' Caroline corrected. ''This is one of those. What is probably more significant here is that we are dealing with a person who is decidedly organized and methodical in his or her thinking. This person needs to be in control of his environment which most likely means that, underneath all of the control and efficiency, this is basically an insecure person. Otherwise, he wouldn't need to be on top of every single detail all the time the way I suspect he does.''

''Interesting. How would someone show that insecurity?''

''He may not show it at all. He may actually have himself and his life under so much control through constant attention to detail that he's been able to hide his basic feelings of inadequacy from the people around him. They may think he's on top of everything and the most confident person they know.''

''How would that relate specifically to this case?'' Mike had set his fork down on the rim of his plate and now listened intently.

''Well, this kind of person can never feel absolutely certain that he has convinced everybody that he's in control and competent. He would live in constant fear of the secret of his true inadequacy coming out. His victims could have threatened exposure of that in some way.''

''I see.'' Mike tapped the rim of his coffee cup, obviously pondering what she had said.

''In fact, the orderliness of the scenes where the bodies have been found could be a form of compensation for the lack of control the murderer is feeling in his present life.''

''You mean that things aren't going well for this guy so he kills people because he's good at it and that makes him feel better about himself?''

Caroline smiled. ''Something like that.''

Mike shook his head and sighed.

''I have some other thoughts, too,'' she said. ''Eat your breakfast before it gets cold, and I'll run down a few more possibilities.''

Mike took up his fork again as Caroline checked the next page in her notebook.

A wave of relief washed over her, as if the fear that had been resting on her shoulders was now being lifted. Mike was actually listening to what she had to say, and without the skepticism she had more than half expected from him. He was treating her like a serious and credible professional person. Her past experience of hometown attitudes toward her had been very different, and she could hardly have been more pleased. When the waitress stopped by to refill their coffee cups, Caroline favored her with a smile so brilliant the woman couldn't help but respond in kind.

''Now for one of my more imaginative theories,'' Caroline began. ''It has to do with the state of the places where the bodies are discovered. It's possible that the killer romanticizes the murders by removing all signs of struggle or blood. He pretties up the scene to make it, in his mind, more socially acceptable. He may have done the same thing with some of the more sordid details of his own life. In fact, he may have invested considerable energy in keeping what he thinks of as his shameful family secrets from being revealed.''

"That's imaginative all right," Mike said. "But it makes some sense, too."

"He doesn't necessarily want notoriety for his crimes, like some pattern killers who have made themselves conspicuous in the media by leaving notes or calling the press."

"I'd thought about that," Mike said, putting his coffee cup down. "It's almost as if he might be kind of a shy person, who keeps to himself and does these murders because he can't stop himself."

"But that doesn't mean he's not proud of them. He could also be compensating for a life of failures by trying to commit the perfect crime."

Mike sighed. "That would fit Lester Pickett to a tee. From what I can tell, he hasn't been able to win for losing since he was a kid. I wouldn't say he has the kind of orderly life you're talking about, though. He strikes me as somebody who's just barely making it. One thing could knock him completely out of control."

"That could work here, too. If he needs that control and feels it always in jeopardy, the one thing that knocks him over the edge could cause a very strong reaction. It might even turn him violent. Remember that these things are happening beneath the surface of the conscious mind. A person can appear to be a fairly simple sort on the outside and still have some pretty complicated emotions boiling inside."

"He does have a history of getting into barroom scraps every so often. Nothing too serious, but they happen."

"That could be a pattern of his frustration building up and coming to a head periodically. Did he actually injure people?"

"According to his yellow sheet, he broke a guy's jaw once."

"I see," Caroline said as she scribbled that down in her notebook.

"Let me ask you something. How sure can we be that these theories will really apply?"

Caroline looked at him a moment before answering. "We can't be absolutely sure of anything. Psychology isn't an exact science, and we don't have much to go on with just two cases to analyze. All I can give you are directions and possibilities. If you expect more than that, you need a fortune-teller."

Mike reached across the table and put his hand over hers. "I don't need anybody but you," he said, his eyes boring into hers and challenging her to look away.

The intensity of his gaze startled. She stared back helplessly, hardly breathing, as if caught in a magic, magnetic beam that held her in his spell.

"Is there anything more I can get for you folks?"

The waitress was standing over the table, glancing from one of them to the other with a quizzical expression on her face.

Caroline pulled her hand from beneath Mike's and began gathering up her notes and folders. She couldn't bring herself to look up at the waitress, who would be certain to see the bright flush Caroline could feel on her cheeks.

"I'll take the check," Mike said, sounding much more self-contained than Caroline was feeling.

She was not pleased by the way he could throw her off balance with a simple move like touching her hand and staring into her eyes. She had wanted him to see her as a serious professional, but she wasn't at all sure she could trust herself to *act* like a professional when she *re*acted so strongly just to being near him.

"Is that it for the theories?" Mike asked.

Caroline's mind had gone blank for the moment except for her concerns about the way he made her feel when they were together. Now she forcibly reordered her thinking.

"There's one more possibility," she said. "The killer may be creating some kind of message with these murders and challenging you to interpret what it is, like a puzzle to solve."

"Or the truth could be something much more straightforward, and whoever is killing these guys has simply been challenged or threatened by them in some way. Right?"

"Right," said Caroline, tapping the folders and notes together into a neat pile. "They could be loose ends he has to get rid of. Then, of course, you have to find a way to connect him personally to each of the victims."

"That might be possible with the two we have already," Mike mused almost to himself, "but if there are more killings to come, it might get harder and harder to make a personal connection for every one."

"Exactly," Caroline said, getting ready to leave.

"Let me walk you back to your room," Mike said, pulling out his wallet and a bill to leave by his plate.

"No!" Caroline said a bit too adamantly. "I—I have some things to take care of in town." The last thing she wanted was a repeat of what had happened when he'd walked her to her room yesterday.

"Then I'll give you a lift wherever you're going."

"It would be more convenient to use my own car," she said, and she managed what she hoped was a businesslike smile despite the fact that he was throwing her off balance again.

"Of course," he said politely.

"Oh, my heavens. I almost forgot something very important," she said, unnerved that he had put her in such disarray that she couldn't seem to think straight. "The files on the first victim mentioned that Tim Manders was at the scene where the body was found."

"That's right. He found the John Doe and called it in."

Caroline had begun to walk between the tables toward the exit. She wanted to make this one point, then escape from the uneasiness that she inevitably felt in Mike's presence.

"I knew Tim when we were both growing up here, and I've heard things about him since. He could fit the description of somebody whose life is and has been a little out of control. Even back in high school he had some strange habits."

"Like what?"

"Well, he was known for sneaking into bathrooms at parties when he knew there was a girl in there."

"Did he ever do that with you?"

Caroline laughed. "No, my mother didn't let me go to parties very often."

"I remember that your mom kept a pretty tight rein on you," Mike said.

"Yes, she did," Caroline said, suddenly wishing she hadn't let the conversation stray into the dangerous territory of their mutual past.

"Can we go somewhere and talk some more?" Mike asked. "About the Manders angle, I mean?"

That was the last thing Caroline wanted. She'd kept herself on top of her feelings quite admirably to this point, but she wasn't sure how much longer she could sustain that effort. She was about to remind him that she had things to do in town when she was saved by the blessed *bleep-bleep* of his beeper.

Mike pressed a button to stop the sound. "I have to get this," he said. "But before I go, I want to ask you one thing."

Caroline held her breath.

"In these . . . bathroom incidents, did Manders ever do anything to the girls involved?"

Caroline was relieved. "From what I heard, all he wanted to do was watch."

"Still, we may have enough to put him on the list right next to Pickett," Mike said.

"I wouldn't rule either of them out entirely at this point."

"I'm also interested in talking with you some more about the possibility of the killer being a woman."

Something in the way he said that made her wonder what he was thinking and why she got the feeling it had particular significance for her.

When he excused himself to go to a phone in the hotel lobby, she made her escape out the side door into the parking lot.

Caroline didn't go to her car. She had fabricated that story about things to do. She hurried across the lot to the side entrance that led to her hallway and her room. And she realized in amazement that she was running away from Mike Schaeffer

INVESTIGATE THE two homicides some more. Connect either Pickett or Manders to both of them with a solid body of evidence. Take him in. No more murders. That was how Mike was hoping this case would go. This morning's beeper call had put an end to any such fantasy.

The third victim was only a little heftier than the other two had been. Maybe it hadn't been as easy to cover up the drag marks from this one. Under the surface of reordered brush, the zigzag, parallel pattern of two heels could be seen clearly in places. Or the killer might have been in more of a hurry this time, afraid of being caught.

"Or maybe he's getting too confident for his own good." Palumbo noted the third possibility. "That could be what will bring him down in the end."

"Let's hope it brings him down soon," Mike said, staring down at the old man on the riverbank.

They were back along Black River again, but much farther east than the scene of the first discovery and all the way out Huntington Street near Sewall's Island. It would have been deserted here last night when the body was dumped. The killer wasn't taking any chance of being caught. Each discovery site was more remote than the last but still in a place where somebody would readily find the victim in the daytime.

Once again, the victim was a known alcoholic, a habitual visitor at the county jail several miles back west along this same river. He was better dressed than his two predecessors, and this person had a family he lived with between stints in the alleyways around town. In fact, he had a sister, as Mike remembered, who had never given up hope of reforming her wayward brother one day. She'd be heartbroken to learn there was no chance of that salvation now. Mike would have to do that duty. Such house calls were about his least favorite part of the job.

"Make sure they go over this one with a microscope. Don't let them miss a thing. I want to see a pile of plastic pouches like never before," Mike said, referring to the samples of lint, hair, nail parings and so forth the forensic people would collect.

"You got it, boss," Palumbo said, watching Mike closely.

He didn't generally sound so angry about a case, but then, there weren't many cases that offered as few leads as these three did. There also weren't that many cases up here that brought out the downstate press the way this one was beginning to. A stringer from a Syracuse paper was already at this scene, trying her best to wangle her way past the squad car cop who was keeping onlookers back from the body.

Maybe she was the one who'd coin the term Dead Drunk Murders that would appear in the next edition. The pressure after that would be hot and heavy from a lot of sources, and Mike would be the principal target. Maybe that was why he was acting so sore this morning. Or maybe he just plain didn't like having to admit there could be a serial killer at work on his turf.

CAROLINE WAS STARTLED by the phone ringing. Very few people knew she was here, and that was the way she wanted it.

Of course, one person knew Caroline was here in the north country and just where she could be found. Mike Schaeffer.

Oddly, she felt a strong twinge of disappointment when she heard another man's voice at the other end of the line.

"My name is Nate Conklin," he said. "I understand you've been out at my house looking for Willow Fowler."

"I—I, yes, I was," Caroline stammered. Was she going to have a charge of break-and-enter to contend with now along with everything else? "I'm sorry about that. I know I shouldn't have gone inside when no one was home, but I was so worried about Willow that—"

"I'm worried about her, too," Mr. Conklin interrupted. "Can I come to your room so we can talk about that? I'm out in the lobby on the house phone."

Caroline automatically gave him her room number, then wished she had arranged to meet him in the coffee shop. She didn't know this man. But before she could suggest that he had hung up and was apparently on his way to her room. She swept stray items of underwear and jewelry into the top drawer of the dresser and wondered what had she gotten herself into, anyway. She'd come up here to lend a simple helping hand to a friend. She hadn't bargained on the complicated psychodrama she found herself in the midst of now.

When she opened her hotel-room door, she knew instantly why Willow might have preferred Nate Conklin's company to that of her husband on occasion. He was blond and so deeply tanned that he must not mind the chill of this summer. His eyes glinted a sincere, worried blue, and she could tell from the look in them that she had nothing to fear from this man. All he had on his mind right now was Willow, and he was even more worried than Caroline about what might have happened.

"Come in," Caroline said.

He brushed past her and into the room and started talking immediately.

"I don't think she just took off like Della says." He paced back and forth in front of the dresser. "I think he did something to her."

"You mean Justin?" Caroline was reminded of the way Willow had flitted nervously up and down the same path her friend Nate was taking now.

"Of course, I mean Justin." Nate apparently heard the impatience in his own voice and stopped his pacing to turn toward her. "I'm sorry. I don't mean to be rude. I'm just worried about Willow."

"I understand," Caroline said. "I'm worried about her, too."

"Then you have to believe me about Justin. She told me all about the way he's been with her, following her around and making threats."

"She told me, too," Caroline said.

"I never should have left town," he said, beginning to pace again. "I knew she was getting more and more upset by him even though she tried to hide it from me."

"Have you been in regular touch with Willow since she married Justin?"

Nate spun around. "It isn't what you think. It isn't what everybody in this damned, small-minded town thinks. We're friends. That's all. That's all Willow lets us be. I might want more than that between us, but she has never let me forget for one minute that she has a husband and she intends to stay faithful to him whether he deserves her fidelity or not."

"I believe you," Caroline said.

"Look, Caroline," he said, sounding a bit calmer. "Willow has told me a lot about you and what good friends the two of you are. If she's told you about Justin's obsessiveness toward her, then you must have the same questions I have about her disappearance."

"Do you really think she's disappeared? Everybody else seems to think she's taken off on her own for a couple of days. Her housekeeper, even Della."

"Della has no idea what's going on between Willow and Justin."

"As I remember it, Willow always told her mother everything, especially the important things. Why not this?" It was a question she'd asked herself, as well.

Nate leaned toward her. "Willow didn't tell her mother this because she didn't want to disappoint her."

At Caroline's quizzical expression, he went on to explain. "You see, Della used to worry about Willow a lot before she got married. Then when Justin came along, Della stopped worrying. She thought he was a prize catch and exactly what Willow needed. I think that may have been part of the reason Willow married him—because Della wanted it so much. When the marriage started going wrong, Willow didn't have the heart to tell her mother the truth. That's why Della still thinks they're the perfect couple and Justin can do no wrong.''

''That would explain Della's attitude, but how do you account for the high opinion so many other people in town seem to have of him?''

Nate brought his clenched fists down hard against his thighs. ''That's the most frustrating part of this. Fowler's got everybody fooled. He's a con artist, and they've been conned. That's all there is to it.''

''Everyone he knows? That's not such an easy feat,'' Caroline said cautiously, knowing it was, nonetheless, possible.

''I was skeptical myself when Willow first came to me, but after a while I changed my mind. I know her pretty well, and I don't think she'd make up the things she said he did to her.''

Nate turned and took hold of Caroline's shoulders. The pleading in his eyes echoed in his voice. ''I truly believe that there's a side to this man that wants to own Willow body and soul, like she was a pet puppy or a work of art. When she tried to get a little freed of that, he couldn't stand it. He clamped down on her. And there's no telling what he'd do if he thought she was about to leave him altogether. That's what she was planning to do, wasn't it?''

''She was planning to go away the morning after I saw her last.''

Nate raised both hands. ''You see what I mean? He must have found out what she was up to and done something to stop her.''

"Do you think she would have asked you to join her?"

Caroline had to know the answer to that, no matter what.

He sighed. "I wish that were the case. She made it very clear that, if she ever got herself out of this marriage of hers, the last thing she wanted was to hook up with another man, at least not for some time to come."

"How did you feel about that?" Caroline asked.

"I made it just as clear that, when she was ready to hook up again, I'd still be waiting."

The sincerity in his eyes bespoke the truth.

"Then let's respect what I know Willow would want, and not do anything rash. Let's put this in the hands of the authorities. I think they're the ones to handle it now," she suggested.

She felt a moment's satisfaction. At least now she had something more than just her own word to go on. Mike would have to listen to what she had to say about Willow this time.

Chapter Eleven

Caroline's first surprise came when she discovered that Mike wasn't on duty. He seemed always to be working, but right now he was at home having lunch. Her next surprise was that the desk sergeant was willing to give out Mike's home address. The sergeant said he knew she was a special friend of the captain's so it would be all right.

"Special friend?" What did that mean, and why did the sergeant think she was one? Were she and Mike the subject of station house scuttlebutt?

What didn't surprise her was the address itself. She remembered it all to well. The sergeant began to give her directions, but she thanked him and said she knew the way.

"Are you sure?" he asked. "It's pretty confusing up that way."

"I'm sure," she said and thanked him again.

The part of town where Mike lived might have been confusing to a lot of people. This area of compact brick homes had been built in the housing boom following World War II, when it had apparently been thought quaint to have the roads meander in semicir-

cles and odd turnings instead of in straight streets and
avenues like most of the rest of the city. Once off
Washington Street just past the high school, it would
be easy to get lost, especially since many of the houses
looked so much alike.

None of that was a problem for Caroline. She simply took the same route she had traveled countless
times on her bicycle when she was a girl, making the
trip without a single hesitation or wrong turn, and
soon she was pulling up in front of the house where
Mike's family had lived all those years ago when she
would bike past nearly every day just to see if his car
was in the driveway.

She could hardly believe it when a tear came to the
corner of her eye at the sight of the place. She hadn't
realized this particular memory would be so poignant. She wondered if it would have affected her this
way had she not been so closely in touch with Mike
and her feelings about him these past few days. She
also wondered if she might be making a serious mistake, visiting him here like this. If she couldn't handle
being alone with him in her impersonal hotel room,
how was she going to manage being alone with him in
a place so full of her past fantasies?

Any hope of acting on her second thoughts and
getting out of there was dashed as the front door
opened and Mike came bounding down the sidewalk.
He tapped on the passenger's side window, and she
had no choice but to roll it down. He leaned in, smiling from ear to ear.

"What a nice surprise," he said. "You're just in
time for lunch."

"I'm here on business," she said, feeling, as she had this morning, that she had to set parameters right away.

"Then we'll make it a business lunch. We had a business breakfast, now a business lunch. How about a business dinner?"

He winked at her, and if he hadn't been head and shoulders inside the car, she might have gunned the engine and screeched out of there, the way he used to do back in the days when he had a souped-up Mustang convertible that just happened to be the same color as this sports model of hers.

Mike led her into the house and into the kitchen. "Chicken soup," he said. "One of my specialties. I don't usually make it this time of year, but this is one summer you need something to warm your bones. Have a taste."

He held a ladle toward her, and she let him put it to her lips and tip it till she swallowed. She hoped the gesture didn't feel as intimate to him as it did to her.

"Delicious," she said. "You're a good cook."

"You should taste my roast turkey," he said, wiping his hands on his jeans. "I'd make some woman a great husband."

He winked again, but this one was even more unsettling than the one at curbside had been. Caroline decided to turn the topic immediately to business and keep it there.

"I have additional evidence that something may have happened to Willow," she said. "That's why I'm here."

"Really?" He stirred the pot one more time, then replaced the lid. "Exactly what kind of evidence do you have?"

"The kind that you should take very seriously."

"I see," he said in what she had to concede was a serious tone. "Then let's sit down and listen to what you have."

He indicated the table and two cushioned bench seats in the window. They'd called it the breakfast-nook in the old days. Without even thinking about it, Caroline slid into the side she had always taken as a girl. The view from the window was the same—the Schaeffer lawn beyond the flowers that bordered the house, the hedge that hid the driveway, then across into the next property with its lawn neatly mowed like the rest on this quiet block and the quiet blocks surrounding it.

The sky was white with cloud cover that hid the sun and gave a subdued look to the day. Caroline hadn't really noticed that on her way here. She'd been too absorbed by anticipation of driving down this street again, seeing this house again, maybe even sitting in this spot again. The years fell away, and impressions assailed her, snippets of past time when she had sat here back then with Mike's younger sister Judy across the table. They hadn't shared confidences or been close as cousins, the way Willow and Caroline were. She and Judy had done homework together mostly. Judy was only a so-so student and grateful for the help. She had hinted that she knew Caroline's real reason for being here but didn't press the point, probably not wanting to lose the chance of free tutoring by someone with straight-A grades.

Caroline was considering the question of her real reason for being here now. Did it truly have much to do with Willow's problems? Then Mike repeated his question about the nature of Caroline's evidence.

"I have the testimony of someone close to Willow," she said, wondering if she should have used the word *close*. "He also thinks she might be the victim of foul play."

"Is this man anyone I would know?"

"Yes, as a matter of fact, he is." Caroline remembered Mike's flash of what had looked a lot like jealousy. "It's Nate Conklin."

"I see." Mike had been leaning forward slightly to listen. Now he eased back against the seat cushion.

His "I see" struck her the quintessential noncommittal comment.

"What exactly do you see?"

"I see that Nate Conklin has what you might call a special agenda where Willow Fowler is concerned."

"And what do you mean by that?"

"I mean he has personal priorities that could affect his judgment. Say, how about a bowl of soup? I promise you, it's the best chicken soup you'll be offered today."

"No, thank you. What personal priorities would you be referring to?"

Mike sighed. "I guess there's no way to avoid getting into this. Nate is in love with Willow."

"That wouldn't necessarily make his judgment any less reliable. It might make him more attuned to her and her true situation."

"If love was as far as he carried it, that might be true. Come on, Caro. Can't I interest you in a bowl of soup?'' Mike smiled at her in a way that showed how hard he was trying to divert her from the subject.

''I didn't come here for lunch, Mike. I came here because I want to know what has happened to my friend. Now, are you going to explain that last remark about Nate?''

''All right, all right. No more attempts to lure you with my cooking prowess.'' He must have seen her knit her brows, because he changed his tone from playful to serious once more. ''It's very simple really. Nate loathes Justin Fowler, and he's bad-mouthed him to a lot of people. I'm surprised Justin hasn't taken him to court for slander.''

''Maybe Nate is right about Justin.''

''Come on, Caro,'' Mike said for a second time. ''Do you really think a man as visible as Justin could be some kind of Bluebeard without anybody knowing it?''

''Nate Conklin seems to know it.''

''Look, Caro. I realize that terrible things can happen in families behind closed doors, and nobody outside suspects a thing. But I honestly don't believe that's what's happening with Willow and Justin.''

''What do you believe is happening then?''

Caroline sounded indignant despite herself. She had to admit she still didn't have much of a case against Justin. And after all, the people around here were much closer to the day-to-day situation and the individuals involved. Was it arrogant of her to assume she knew more about what was going on than they did?

''I think Willow is restless in her marriage and wants out, and she's creating a smoke screen for following through with that desire.''

"Why would she do that?"

"If she can make Justin out to be the villain, it would put her in a stronger position when it comes time for the courts to determine the divorce settlement."

"You mean you think Willow would do this for money? That doesn't sound a thing like the Willow I know!"

"Maybe it doesn't sound like the Willow you used to know, but Justin has introduced her to a pretty high-priced life-style since then. She seems to like it a lot, too."

Caroline thought about Willow's expensive clothes and the elegant decor of her home. Still, that didn't make her a mercenary. She loved beautiful things, true, but she'd never sell her soul for them.

"You seem to have dismissed my arguments as usual," she said, sliding out of the bench and standing up. "I'm sorry I bothered you."

"You didn't bother me," Mike said, rising also. "You could never bother me. Except in very nice ways, of course." He looked down into her eyes. "Won't you stay for lunch?"

"I have to go, Mike. I have things to do."

"I see."

There it was again. But this time he was right in not committing himself to believing what she'd said. She had nothing planned to do. She simply wanted to get out of there and away from his disturbing, frustrating presence.

"Then I guess you'd better get on with your busy afternoon," he said. "Maybe some other time."

The spicy aroma from the pot on the stove was tantalizing, and so was Mike, in his close-fitting jeans and white T-shirt. His thick brown hair glinted chestnut, and his gray eyes seemed so deep she could fall into them.

Almost all of Caroline wanted to stay, but the part that was still sane managed to say, "Yes, maybe another time."

"By the way, there's been a third body found," Mike said as he followed her to the front door. "Same m.o. as the other two."

That stopped her for a moment, but she was almost out of here now and determined not to linger for any reason. "I'm sorry to hear it, but until you send me the details, I really can't add anything to what I said this morning at breakfast."

And with that she brushed past him and out the door.

IF ONLY she could find a witness Mike would consider reliable where Willow was concerned. Caroline almost wished she could give up on the whole thing, pack her bags and head back to Westchester, where she belonged. Instead, she was quite possibly making a fool of herself over a missing person who might not be missing at all.

Still, until she was absolutely certain what had or had not happened to Willow, Caroline knew she couldn't get out of here and go back home where life suddenly seemed much less complicated than it had a few days ago. If she could only come up with that objective witness.

Then it struck her, so hard she nearly swerved out of her lane of traffic. Willow had mentioned a man from the unemployment office who had driven her home and witnessed the scene Justin had made. Caroline headed for the county offices.

The waiting room was packed with disgruntled and desperate-looking people. After endless maneuvering through bureaucratic red tape, she was finally directed to the desk of the man who had handled Willow's job application.

Unfortunately, from the first mention of Willow, Mark Perkins made it abuntantly clear that he did not want to get involved.

"I had nothing to do with that lady then, and I've got nothing to do with her now," he said. "But, off the record, that husband of hers is a crazy man. I feel sorry for her for having to live with him, but I'm no hero. I'm keeping strictly out of it."

"What do you mean he's a crazy man?"

"We were just sitting there in the car talking— nothing else, I swear. He comes up, yanks open the door and pulls her out. I mean, this guy was out of control. I thought he was going to haul off and punch her right there in the street. I never saw anybody so crazy mad in my life."

"Anything else?"

"Well, there were the things she said in the interview, about how she lost her job because he locked her up in the house and wouldn't let her out for days."

"Did you think she was telling the truth?"

"I checked with her former employer. They said that was the same story she'd told them, and they'd thought she was making it up. I would've thought that, too. I mean her husband's a well-respected guy around here. Who would have thought? But then I saw him in action, and now I believe every word she said about him was true."

Caroline wanted to hug him. Here was her objective witness! Now if only she could get him to cooperate with the authorities. "What happened that day, after Mr. Fowler pulled his wife out of the car?"

"I took off as soon as I could get the car in gear. No way was I going to stick around long enough to find out what that maniac husband of hers had in mind for me."

"Mrs. Fowler is a dear friend of mine, and I'm afraid she might be in deep trouble. Won't you reconsider telling this story to the police?" Caroline asked.

"Are you kidding?"

Up to that moment, they had kept their voices low so the occupants of the surrounding desks wouldn't hear, but Mark's last exclamation came out so loud it turned several heads.

"Are you kidding?" he repeated, nearly whispering this time. "First of all, if it gets out that I was, what they call, fraternizing with a client, I could lose my job. Worse than that, I'd be tangling with Justin Fowler. Even if he wasn't squirrelly, he has too many friends in this town. I've got nothing to do but lose if I mess with him *or* his wife. You can count me out on that one."

Caroline nearly wept. But what else could she expect from a man who had left a woman in an obviously violent situation and run off to save his own skin? A Sir Lancelot Mark Perkins wasn't. She thanked him for his time and headed dispiritedly back through the waiting room, which was still packed with desperate people.

HER TALK WITH Mark Perkins had accomplished one thing Caroline decided. She now knew two independent sources confirming that Willow had been telling the truth about Justin. Unfortunately, that fed her fears that Willow could be in big trouble right now, and that her own well-respected husband could be the cause. She was all but certain that what Justin had been saying about Willow was patently untrue. But she still had no real proof. None she could use, anyway. She was also fresh out of leads.

Justin was her last resort.

"CAROLINE! What a lovely surprise. Any friend of my wife is always more than welcome here," Justin Fowler greeted her in his elegant office.

Caroline smiled back, though she found his effusiveness unconvincing. "Justin, I'm still not comfortable in my mind about what may be going on with Willow. I hoped we could talk about that."

"Of course, we can talk, if that'll make you feel better. But there is nothing going on with her, I assure you. Willow has merely taken one of her occasional vacations. She's probably having a high old time for herself somewhere right now. I'm the only one to suffer from these little jaunts of hers." He hung his head in what looked like sincere distress, but Caroline still wasn't convinced.

"Does she know you feel this way about these absences of hers?"

"I've certainly told her enough times. Unfortunately, consideration of the feelings of others isn't among my wife's virtues."

"I've always known Willow to be very considerate. She takes after Della that way."

"Willow has changed since you knew her, Caroline. She is hardly her mother's sweet, innocent daughter anymore."

"I see," Caroline said. "How long do you think Willow will be gone?"

Justin hesitated a moment, his fingers steepled.

"May I confide in you?" He leaned toward her across his desk.

"I wish you would."

"I haven't told this to anyone...." He hung his head for a moment once again, sorely testing Caroline's patience with what increasingly impressed her as his theatrics. "I...have a terrible suspicion that Willow...that Willow might not come back this time."

His voice was resonant with heartbreak, but his words had struck a chill down Caroline's spine. If Willow never came back, it could be because Justin had made certain she wasn't able to.

Caroline forced herself to remain calm. Don't get ahead of yourself, she thought. No jumping to scary conclusions until they're warranted. Still, she would need to exercise extreme caution with Justin Fowler.

After making the appropriate commiserating noises and assuring him that certainly his wife would come back to him, she rose to leave. Justin, however, insisted on walking her to her car.

He stopped to admire it before opening her door.

"Quite the sporty model," he said. "Is this yours or a rental?"

"It's mine," she said, getting in and starting the engine, anxious to get away from him.

"Sounds powerful. How was the mileage driving up here?"

"Good," she said. "It gets good mileage." That wasn't true. This car was a gas guzzler, especially at highway speeds, but she wanted him to stop talking and let her go.

"When was it that you got here?" he asked, continuing his infuriating small talk.

"Saturday night," she said, shoving the gearshift into reverse. "I got here Saturday night."

"Too bad you've spent so much of your visit worrying needlessly about Willow. I don't imagine you'll be able to stay much longer. That successful business of yours must be needing you back soon."

So that was the reason for all this chitchat. He was pumping her about how long she was going to stay.

Though her better judgment should have prompted her to agree, her anger for Willow prompted her to put him on notice that she wasn't going anywhere. "My partner is prepared to manage things without me for as long as is necessary," she said. And she let out the clutch and eased herself out of the parking space.

Chapter Twelve

Caroline was walking across the parking lot toward the rear door of her hotel when she heard a car door slam behind her. A small knot of fear tightened her stomach in response, but it was broad daylight, so she told herself to stop being silly. She did walk faster though, especially when she heard footsteps gaining on her. Could Justin have followed her from his office? That thought made her walk faster.

"Hey, what's your rush?"

Caroline sighed and stopped in her tracks. It was Mike. Then he was next to her, smiling down in that winning way she found so hard to resist.

"When did you take to skulking around parking lots?" she asked.

"In my business we call it surveillance of the subject under suspicion."

"Suspicion of what?"

"Suspicion of having no plans for dinner."

"What makes you so sure I don't?"

"Because when you came to my house this noon and I mentioned having dinner together, you didn't jump in with an instant refusal." He held the door for her to walk inside. "My observation of your behavior tells me you would not have passed up an opportunity to put me off if there was one."

She stared at him. Had she been that obvious in her attempts to avoid close contact with him?

"Remember, I'm a detective," he said. "Observation is my business."

Caroline smiled and nodded. He was such a disarming man. It was almost impossible to keep her guard constantly in place against him. She was about to walk toward the steps to the lobby when he took her arm.

"I'll be waiting for you in the bar," he said. "You'll probably want to get into something more casual."

She was still wearing the mauve suit. "What, may I ask, am I making this change for?"

"How could you forget?" He spread his hands in mock wonder. "It's Tuesday."

"So?" She was trying not to laugh. She knew she was supposed to be resisting him, but she was finding it more difficult by the second to hold a firm line against him.

"You *have* forgotten. Tuesday is pizza night at Art's. Don't you remember how we all used to go there on Tuesdays?"

Art's was a restaurant on the other side of town. Caroline did recall that they served great pizza and that she'd gone there with the Schaeffers several times as a kid. Then it dawned on her.

"That was Wednesday night," she said. "Wednesday was pizza night at Art's, not Tuesday."

"A technicality. In my business, a technicality often gets one off the hook."

"What if I come up with substantial evidence of manipulation here?"

"I'll be waiting in the bar to hear it," he said and started off in that direction. "So go change and do all that stuff it takes women so long to do in the bathroom," he called over his shoulder.

Caroline opened her mouth to say something in protest, but it was too late.

What were her objections anyway? She didn't want to get any more involved because there could be no real future for them. Their lives and their thinking about things were miles apart, both literally and figuratively. Did that mean she couldn't go out and have an innocent pizza with him? It wasn't as if he'd asked her out for a formal date at some big deal spot. Art's was the most casual place imaginable. At least it always had been, and she doubted it would have changed much.

But could any time spent with Mike Schaeffer on a personal basis end up to be entirely innocent? Weren't her feelings about him already too riled up for that? Hadn't she been warning herself for days now that what she felt for Mike was nothing more than the acting out of a leftover adolescent fantasy?

She had been standing in the corridor near the stairs, and people were beginning to gape at her curiously as they passed by. She walked toward the stairs, more slowly than usual, still debating how to handle this situation. As her foot hit the first step, she knew what she had to do. It was a technique she might have suggested to a patient in therapy.

Since resisting the fantasy was obviously not working, why not try giving in to it? This was the same kind of method that sometimes worked with dream behavior. If a dream was so troubling that it woke you up in terror, you might try deliberately going back into the dream and making it come out with you conquering the source of the terror in the end. Maybe she could apply that principle here with Mike. Maybe she could take control of the fantasy instead of fighting it.

Caroline was so pleased with herself for coming up with a new approach to her dilemma that she didn't think—or she didn't let herself think—about any possible hitches in the plan, such as Mike's winsome ways and the effect they had on her ability to stay in control. Instead, she hurried off toward her room, already intent upon what she should wear for an evening with her fantasy man.

CAROLINE HAD INSISTED that she and Mike take separate cars to Art's. She might be surrendering to fantasy to some extent, but it was still important to maintain the means of keeping in charge of the situation. She was reminded of Della Gilchrist telling her and Willow they should always take "mad money" along on a date—in case they got mad at what was happening and needed taxi fare home. Separate cars were the adult woman's version of mad money.

"What will it be tonight, Mike?" the waitress asked with a friendly smile. "The usual?"

"I see you still come here a lot," Caroline said.

"He's one of our most regular regulars," the waitress answered. "If Mike ever stopped coming here, I swear we'd be headed straight for bankruptcy."

"I can tell he's a favorite."

"Oh, I wouldn't go *that* far," the waitress quipped with a wink at Caroline. "He's just in here a lot."

"If you two are finished talking about me as if I weren't here, I'd like to order now," Mike said. "As a matter of fact, I *won't* have the usual. I'll have what the lady is having, and the lady is having lasagna with extra sauce and a salad on the side."

Caroline stared at him in wonderment.

"Is that right?" the waitress asked her.

"Yes, it is," Caroline answered softly.

That was exactly what she used to order all those years ago when she came here with the Schaeffer family. She could hardly have been more astonished. Most of the men she'd known could barely manage to remember another person's wants or needs for the duration of an evening, much less for years. There was no denying that Mike was something special.

The waitress left to take their order to the kitchen. Art's hadn't changed much, Caroline was glad to see. The decor was still simple and informal. She'd always felt comfortable here, even though she had little experience of restaurants when she was growing up since she and her parents almost never went out together.

The hum of pleasant conversation and friendly laughter still emanated from the surrounding tables. She'd felt that she was in the midst of a warm circle of families back then, and she felt the same way now. It brought a tightness to her throat, and her eyes were suddenly wet, just as they had been the other day when she saw Della Gilchrist again. Caroline marveled at how an occasional dose of family normalcy and caring—like what she had experienced with the Schaeffers and the Gilchrists—had brightened an otherwise bleak adolescence.

"What are you thinking?" Mike asked.

"I'm remembering why I was drawn to family therapy," she said.

"We could certainly use somebody like you to organize some of that around here. The north country is up to its frostbitten ears in family problems, and the screwed up adults who came from families with problems keep passing them on."

"You must run into a lot of that in your work."

"You've got it. And I'd love to have somebody to refer them to. Of course, if you were the therapist, I'd be the first referral I'd make."

"And why would that be?" Caroline asked.

"Hey, in my line of work, I could use a hefty prescription of caring and concern, anyway."

"No prescriptions, Mike. Even when I finish my degree, I'll be a psychologist, not a psychiatrist."

"I'd refer myself to you anyway," he said with a smile that lit an unexpected hint of blue in his gray eyes.

She could feel him taking emotional control, about to begin plucking her heartstrings to his tune. If she was going to give herself up to her fantasy, she supposed she should simply let him pluck away. But something in her wasn't quite ready, so she changed the subject instead.

"I'd rather you refer me any new findings you might have on the murders," she said.

Mike's smile faded. "There's a subject that could ruin even my appetite."

"I take it the investigation isn't going well."

"That's the understatement of the decade."

"What about Lester Pickett?"

"He's still in the running, but we haven't come up with a link to victims one and three."

"That doesn't mean there isn't one. Remember, you're not necessarily dealing with rational behavior here. That means the links may not be obvious in rational terms."

Mike nodded. "I've also put Tim Manders on the short list. He does have the kind of background of frustrations and failures you described in your profile. We did some asking around today and found out he's also been pretty withdrawn and secretive lately."

"I think I know what you mean about his history of frustrations. I remember hearing that his father was pretty hard on him."

"That never stopped from what we've found out. The word around town is that his father let Tim take over the business mostly for the chance to sneer at him when he failed."

"Mr. Manders, senior, sounds like a really nice guy," Caroline said sarcastically.

"The best thing he ever did for Tim was retire to Florida. I guess the old man preferred to do his sneering on the beach."

"Have you questioned Tim further?"

"We went over there this afternoon, but he left town on business this morning, so we missed him," Mike said. "I'll catch him as soon as he gets back. I intend to pin him down about what he was doing in that part of town the morning he supposedly found the first body."

"What about the other two nights? Do you have any idea where he was then?"

"I'll find out when he gets back."

Before Mike could continue, the waitress arrived carrying two steaming plates heaped with lasagna in a thick red sauce. Caroline had forgotten how big the servings were. Had she really been able to eat this much when she was younger?

"I hope you enjoy it," said the waitress as she set down their salads.

"I'm sure I will," said Caroline, and she wasn't just being polite. It smelled delicious.

She made a fair dent in the oblong of pasta before looking up to resume the conversation. When she did, she saw that Mike was watching her with a smile on his face.

"I like a woman with a healthy appetite," he said.

A blush sprang to her pale cheeks as she considered the other appetites he'd had the opportunity to admire in her. She lowered her head and wondered how much control she was going to be able to maintain over this reality version of her fantasy.

"The cool weather must have made me hungry," she said. She took a moment to smooth the napkin in her lap and compose herself. "So," she said at last, "Have you any new leads at all?"

"As a matter of fact, I do. It was Palumbo who came up with it, and I think he may have something."

"Can you tell me about it?"

"As long as we're still . . . colleagues, I can." Mike stared deep into her eyes.

"Well, we are still working together."

"There's a local character most people call The Preacher. His real name is Parnell Janeway. He has a fanatical hatred of drunkards. He preaches against them, rousts them out of barrooms when he can get away with it, harasses them on the street. He even went so far as to circulate a petition to have anybody guilty of public drunkenness put out of town. Believe it or not, he got some people to sign it. Then he took it to the city council, several times. They kept voting it down, and he kept going back."

"That would certainly suggest a motive, but would he carry it to the point of murder?"

"That was what I wondered—till Palumbo showed me a list of complaints against Janeway. It seems he's been getting more violent lately, hitting people, pushing them around. No charges have been pressed or we would have had him in jail by now for assault. There's always the possibility that he could have graduated to killing, maybe by accident at first. He's certainly obsessed, even considers himself the leader of a movement. He calls it his Anti-Dregs Campaign, complete with posters and bumper stickers."

"Do you think he might fit the psychological profile we talked about?"

"I can't be sure yet," Mike said with a hint of desperation.

Caroline understood his mood. She was aware of the growing pressure on him to solve these murders. How long would the town put up with a daily diet of murder in the headlines? She gently changed the subject to the superior quality of the lasagna and kept the talk light from then on throughout a delicious dinner, until the coffee and dessert plates had been cleared and there was nothing left for them to do but go home.

IN ALL THE YEARS of her future, when she looked back on the remaining hours of this momentous night in her life, Caroline would remember every detail of how it happened but not every detail of why it happened. She knew what she felt for Mike as a person. She cared very much about him. Whatever cautions she might resolve to take, no matter how many times she reminded herself that this thing between them had nowhere to go and nothing to do with their present lives, the bottom line was that caring.

She wasn't ready to put a name to what he meant to her, or even to determine whether those feelings were real or merely a remnant of something years-past and unfulfilled, longing for resolution. Did she feel merely affection and closeness for him, or was it something more? She drew a cautionary line against attaching a defining word to her true and deep response whenever she so much as thought of being with him. She knew that once she had spoken such a word, if only in her mind, it would remain spoken forever, never to be denied again.

She wasn't ready for that, but she was ready to listen to Mike with her heart and to hear the discouragement he was feeling beneath his jovial facade throughout dinner. The case wasn't going well, and he was under a lot of pressure to turn that around. Then, to make matters worse, he had tried so hard to get close to her, and she had resisted him at every turn. She had vowed to herself that she would let her emotions take the lead for a change. Then she had spent the entire evening sidestepping and fast-shuffling in a dance that he had to interpret as rejection.

As they were walking back to their cars, she could sense the gloom settling over Mike, despite his best attempts at joviality. The pressure was definitely getting to him. She could see it in the ever-so-slight rounding of his usually square shoulders and the absent look in his eyes, as if he might be staring inside himself into a place that was neither bright nor hopeful.

Maybe that was why she turned to him suddenly, just as they were approaching their individual vehicles, and suggested a nightcap. At his obvious surprise, she took a deep breath and commented that if he could make such wonderful chicken soup, his coffee must be superb. He graciously invited her to his place, and she could see the unspoken question in his eyes.

When they reached the tidy brick Schaeffer house with its neat lawn and shrubbery, Caroline pulled her car into the driveway behind Mike's. The town had a law against all-night street parking. Once again Mike looked at her as if he could hardly believe his eyes, but she only ducked her head and walked toward the house.

Once they were inside, Mike moved toward the kitchen to make the coffee they had supposedly come there for. Caroline touched his arm to stop him. He turned slowly toward her, as if expectant but at the same time fearful of his expectations proving false. She slipped her hand downward to his and clasped it. Then she began to walk toward the stairs. He hesitated only an instant, then followed readily.

At the second-floor landing it was Caroline's turn
to hesitate. She remembered very well the way to the
room that had been Mike's all those years ago, but she
wasn't sure that would be his room still. He must have
read her thoughts because he took the lead now, moving slowly, their hands still clasped, toward the room
that had once belonged to his parents. Caroline was
glad of that. She no longer wanted even the slightest
suggestion that tonight was nothing more than the
acting out of some adolescent fantasy. Suddenly she
understood that tonight must be tonight, here and now
and very real.

The leader once more, she guided Mike to the ma-
ple four-poster bed. The room was bathed in soft
shadow and low light from an outdoor streetlamp. She
saw Mike open his mouth to speak, but she put her
finger gently to his lips to stop him. This was a moment too precious for words.

She stepped away from him and began to remove
her clothes, letting her jacket slip down her arms, then
lifting her top over her head and tossing her hair free.
She undid the fastening of her summer skirt and let it
drop to the floor in ripples of fabric as she slid the
sandals from her feet. She stepped over the rumple of
her clothing and stood before him dressed only in her
delicate silk and lace underthings. Mike was gazing at
her with a tenderness in his eyes like nothing she had
ever seen.

Moments later, they were lying side by side on the
bed, facing, naked and open to each other. She could
see his body in the soft light, and it was wonderful, the
most perfect body she had ever seen, or so it seemed
to her. In fact, if she had stopped to think about it at

that moment, she would have realized that she could
not remember ever having looked upon a man's body
before. There was only Mike. There was only now.
Nothing else existed or ever had existed or ever would.

He reached across the few inches between them and
touched her. He ran his hand over her slowly, as if reassuring himself that she was real and not simply his
half of their fantasy. She couldn't hear him breathing, yet she was almost certain she could hear his heart
pound. Or was that her own?

Then his touch was more insistent, more probing.
She arched against his hand, and, as she had been beyond words moments before, she was now beyond
thought or reason. Something much deeper inside had
thrust her toward him. The skin of her nipples pulled
suddenly so tight they ached and tingled. She grasped
his hand, as she had done the other day in her hotel
room, and moved it toward the aching places, knowing that only his stroking and fondling and then his
kiss could ease the urgency there.

She was now feeling that same urgency in her loins,
but she didn't have to guide him there. He had already drawn his other hand up the inside of her thigh
to the spot where she most wanted his hand to be. She
gasped as he touched her there. She wanted to lift
herself toward him yet again, but she was too over-
whelmed by waves of sensation to move.

Caroline had never been particularly aggressive in
lovemaking. She had never felt inspired to be until that
other day in her hotel room. Now she wished she could
rouse herself to such action yet again, but a lethargy
had overtaken her. Her body was beyond her com-
mand. She wished she could urge him on and pull him

inside her. There was nothing in the world she had ever longed for more.

Instead, she drifted—not near the edge of consciousness, but in another realm of consciousness entirely where she was totally sensual and capable only of feeling, not of acting, while some superior awareness assured her that action or even movement on her part was not necessary no matter how much she might yearn for it. In fact, that awareness told her, she mustn't hurry things. She must let all proceed at this agonizing pace, until the agony had reached its absolute crest and she could tolerate not a single second more.

Her body pleaded from every pore for him to quench the desire that blazed through her and filled her and raced along her skin, searing her with every touch of him. Then, when she knew beyond a breath of doubt that she could bear no more, he came into her, easy at first, then hard, with a strangled cry. He slammed himself against her, and she was at last able to move once more, as she had never moved before, and match her cries to his.

AFTERWARD, Caroline was completely at peace, cradled in the crook of his arm, her lips against his chest. She lay still, every now and then sighing and kissing his skin through its covering of silky hair.

She gradually became aware that she had never felt so completely comfortable with another human being as she did right now with Mike. And for the present, she had not the slightest inclination to question either the future or the past that had led her to this moment. Nothing could have been farther from her mind than past chagrin or potential problems. She was totally contented, and not another reality in the universe mattered more to her than that.

"I've just been thinking about how much I love the way you move," Mike said, breaking the silence. "You never hesitate when you walk. You seem to glide along, always knowing exactly where you're going and what you have to do when you get there. It makes me feel like getting up and following you without even asking where we're headed."

Caroline roused herself enough to reply. "I can't imagine you following anybody without question. You always have such definite ideas of your own about what direction to take."

"That may be true in my work, but not necessarily in other areas of my life." Mike was staring at the shadows on the ceiling as the trees outside the window swayed in the night breeze. "Sometimes I stop dead in my tracks with the most intense feeling that my life is slipping by and I'm missing the point. As if I made a wrong turn somewhere and got hopelessly lost."

Caroline edged closer but didn't speak. She could tell he still had more to say.

"When I'm feeling like that," he went on, "I wish so hard that I could figure out where that wrong turning was. I'd run back there right then, as fast as my legs could carry me." He paused. "When you came here, I thought maybe life had done me a special favor and made that new start possible. But I know you have to go away again soon."

A few hours ago such deeply felt words might have frightened her. Now, they only echoed her own deep feelings of sadness.

"Why didn't you and your wife have children?" she asked.

"I wanted to. Barb was against it. I think she had a feeling, right from the start, that we weren't going to make it, and she didn't want to bring any kids into what might end up a broken home."

"Maybe she couldn't give the marriage a real chance if she started out with doubts like that."

"Barb is a very practical woman. She wasn't sure we would keep on wanting the same things out of life, and she turned out to be right."

"You mean she didn't want to stay in Watertown and you did."

"There was more to it than that. Like I told you the other night, we were always more friends than lovers, and that wasn't enough for her."

"Was it enough for you?"

Mike turned on his side and looked at her for a long moment. "I'd hoped it could be. Now I know how wrong I was."

He kissed her softly on her lips, and the tingle was there again, the beginning of wanting him once more, even after the perfect contentment their loving had made her feel.

"Do you know what?" he asked. "Somebody— your father maybe—should be telling you right about now how completely wrong I am for you."

"My father never spoke up for me or anything else," Caroline said, sorry for this break in her beautiful mood.

"Well, somebody should speak up. Because it's true. We're as different from each other as if you lived in the sea and I lived on the land."

"Wasn't there a fairy tale like that, and didn't they work it out in the end?"

"I don't know much about fairy tales," Mike said with a chuckle. "But I think I heard that one once, and it seems to me that one or the other of them died of a broken heart, or maybe it was both of them."

Caroline stared at the way the light from the window caught in the fine hairs of his chest and made them shimmer softly. "I like my version better," she said.

"You mean, 'Happily ever after'?" he asked quietly.

"That's right."

"Do you really think that happens much outside of fairy tales?"

Caroline touched the shimmer gently, and tears rose in her eyes at the overwhelming tenderness that touch made her feel.

"It should," she said.

Chapter Thirteen

"Nothing ever works out for me!"

Stalking the room from one end to the next for nearly an hour had brought no relief and had finally led to talking out loud to the walls.

"I do everything absolutely right, more right than most people could ever hope for, and what happens? Something always goes wrong, that's what happens."

Maybe throwing something heavy would be temporarily satisfying. But that wouldn't be wise. No need to attract attention. Balling a fist and pounding it against a thigh so hard there would be a bruise in that spot tomorrow would have to do.

"It's always some little thing out of the blue. Something there was no way to plan for."

Was there some way this could have been foreseen?

"No, there wasn't. I did everything exactly right. I know I did. As usual, that wasn't enough. Now trouble's coming. I can feel it." The pounding increased. "I can feel it."

Feel it in this tightness in the head, in the narrowly confined stalking back and forth. Still, going anywhere else to blow off steam was taking too much of a chance.

"That would be playing right into their hands. They want me to come out and show myself. They want me to make a huge mistake, but I'm not going to do that." Careful. That high, unnatural whine could draw attention. "But what am I going to do?"

Another body. There could be another body. The pacing stopped in the middle of a stride.

"Do I dare? It gets riskier every time. They're watching now. I have to get farther out from town before I can dump the body. Then what if they don't find it because it's too far away? I would have gone to all that effort for nothing."

What could be done? They were closing in, their breath hot.

"Wait. I'm in control here. I can handle this thing. I can handle all of them."

But what about this new threat? Could it be handled? If only it would go away. If only...

CAROLINE HAD DRIVEN herself home in the middle of the night. A light misting of rain had made the road shimmer under the streetlights, and she couldn't remember ever experiencing a night half so beautiful. She knew that her mood, fresh from the warm hollow of Mike's bed, was probably influencing the way she saw things, but she didn't care. Accuracy of observation wasn't as important just then as how wonderful she felt and, illusion or not, the certainty that the feeling would never end.

She had gone straight to bed, only stripping to her underwear. Even if it hadn't been so late she wouldn't have taken a shower. She wanted to keep the scent of Mike with her a while longer, at least until the morning. Otherwise, the light of day might have convinced her that something so perfect as last night could only have happened in a dream.

In fact, part of her had been suspecting that might be the case as she wandered in and out of sleep in the gloom created by the heavy window curtains. Then the phone rang. The first ring woke her up only enough to make her wonder what the sound could be. The second ring brought her around to realizing it was the phone. But who would be calling her at this hour? On the third ring she knew the answer. It was Mike.

Her heart thudded as she groped for the receiver. "Don't hang up, my darling," she whispered, afraid to take the time to turn on the bedside lamp for fear of missing him.

Her fingers found the receiver and nearly knocked it out of the cradle in her haste.

"Hello? Mike?" she said when she finally got the thing to her ear.

No one answered, and an instant of panic caught her throat. Could he have hung up because she didn't answer soon enough? Was this the sound of a dead line?

"Mike, are you there?" An edge of trepidation had awakened her at last as for the first time, it occurred to her that someone other than Mike might be calling.

Then she heard it. The sound was unmistakable. Sometimes she wondered if perhaps every woman in the world had heard it—the sound of heavy breathing, slow and raspy and so audible that the person on the other end had to have the mouthpiece against his lips.

Still, several seconds passed before Caroline completed the mental transition this new awareness required of her. Only moments ago she had been deep in a thrall of dreamy thoughts. Now she was being most rudely awakened. The leap from fantasizing about her lover to contending with a phone creep was too wide for even a sharp-minded woman to manage quickly.

Caroline forced herself to think about what were considered the best techniques for handling characters like this. Then, suddenly, she didn't care about techniques. All she knew was that this call had stepped very hard on the last edges of a lovely dream, and she was angry about that.

"Get lost, jerk," she shouted, and slammed the receiver down hard. Then she struggled to unclip the cord from the back of the phone so he wouldn't be able to call her again.

But then again, if he couldn't call her, neither could Mike, she fretted. Maybe she should call the front desk.

Wait a minute.

Caroline sat straight up in bed. She had almost forgotten she was in a hotel. That meant whoever had just called her had had to be forwarded through the hotel switchboard. That also meant this wasn't the usual breather who had dialed a number or picked a name at random from the phone book. This caller had to know her name and where to find her.

Caroline liked the feeling even less that this harasser was someone who had targeted her deliberately and personally.

But why? Since sexual harassment of any kind was about power rather than sex, people who did things like this were after a reaction that would make them feel powerful. The more fearful the reaction, the more powerful they would feel.

So somebody was trying to scare her. But who? And why? Unless she was simply jumping to conclusions and this was some kind of joke. But who would consider impersonating a pervert funny? Certainly not Mike.

Caroline pushed the cord back into the phone, lifted the receiver and punched the button for the front desk. The operator sounded sleepy when she answered.

"This is Caroline Hardin. Someone just called for me a couple of minutes ago. Was it a man or a woman?"

"I beg your pardon?" Now she sounded sleepy and confused.

Caroline repeated the question and found out her suspicions had been correct. The caller was a man.

"Did you by any chance recognize the voice?" she asked.

"No, I didn't. Is there something wrong, Miss Hardin?" The operator was suddenly much more alert.

"Nothing I can't handle. Thanks very much."

Caroline hung up the phone and was about to unplug it again but stopped. She supposed she could ask the operator to take messages on all her calls, but that seemed drastic after only one incident. In the golden

glow of the bedside lamp the anxiety the breather had
made her feel seemed more remote by the minute. She
had just about convinced herself not to give any more
thought to the matter when the phone rang again—
and once more someone was breathing into her ear yet
again.

LATER CAROLINE would admit that those phone calls
set her up to react the way she did to the two other
things that happened to her that morning, but that
didn't make them any less real. After checking at the
desk to confirm that the second caller had sounded
like the same man as the first, Caroline dressed quickly
and went out to her car. She didn't want to stay in her
room another minute, and any appetite she might have
had for breakfast was gone. A morning drive seemed
like a bracing alternative.

As she went to unlock her car door she realized it
wasn't locked after all. She removed the key and
opened the door, staring in surprise.

She never left her car unlocked. Of course, she had
been in what she could only describe as a euphoric
state when she got back here from Mike's house in the
wee hours of the morning. Still she was almost certain she had locked the car before going into the hotel. Locking up was habitual with her, as it was with
everybody living so near a big city. And her knowledge of human behavior told her that in a preoccupied state an individual was more likely to perform
habitual tasks automatically than to deviate from
them.

But if she'd locked this car door, how could it be
open now? She was the only one with a key, and she

knew for certain that the other door hadn't been unlocked since the night she drove Willow to Burrville. Caroline had checked it the night that guy chased her on the motorcycle. There hadn't been any reason to unlock or open that door since.

She slid into the car, closed the door and examined it. The window was rolled down barely an inch from the top. She had done that on her way back from Mike's. She had been so delighted by the rainy mist and the enchanted way it made everything look that she had wanted to smell the scent of it, as well. She had rolled the window down just a little, despite the chill. She'd had her own inner warmth going for her last night.

Caroline reminded herself to stay on track and not drift off into daydreams. She needed to keep sharp and figure out what was going on here. At least she understood now how somebody could have opened her door. She didn't remember rolling that window back up when she got here and that meant all anybody would have needed was a wire coat hanger and enough street savvy to straighten it out and fish for the lock through the window crack. This car didn't have any safeguards to prevent that.

She checked the glove compartment, but nothing was missing. Nor did it appear to have been rifled through. In fact, the folded maps and manuals seemed to be in better order than usual. She looked in the back seat and didn't notice anything out of the ordinary at first. Then it struck her.

She had leaned over the driver's seat and was staring at the car floor behind, trying to register what she was seeing. It made so little sense.

Helena was forever teasing her about her car interior being the one area of disorder Caroline allowed herself. There were always various items on the floor—candy wrappers, a professional journal or two, that kind of thing. Especially in the back, where she was less likely to notice the debris.

She was noticing it now—precisely because it wasn't there. She recalled tossing things back here during her trip up north a few days ago. Now they were gone. The dark gold carpeted space was completely clean. Not so much as a bit of lint remained.

Caroline slid back down into the driver's seat and stared at the dashboard, trying to retrace her steps over the last few days. She hadn't been to a car wash lately, so she was fairly sure the usual mess had been in here yesterday. In fact, she had picked up a local paper and left that in the back as well. That was gone now, too.

There was only one explanation that she could think of, and it was totally bizarre. Somebody had broken into her car and cleaned it up for her, even straightening out the stuff in the glove compartment. Why on earth would anybody do that?

She pondered the odd scenario for a moment, and one explanation came to mind, chilling her to the bone.

Whoever had done this had had a single purpose in mind. He had wanted her to know he had been here. There might have been more blatant ways to scare her, but the subtlety of this one did the job beautifully.

Suddenly, the prospect of driving appealed to her far less than it had a few moments ago.

CAROLINE WAS SHAKEN when she got back to her room. That was probably why she knocked over the wastebasket. The contents spilled out onto the floor. She was almost going to leave them there, crawl back into bed and pull the covers up to her chin. She would grab the remote control for the television set and find the most inane, mind-numbing program possible to lull her into blessed oblivion.

Instead, she ran to the telephone and yanked out the cord. At least she wouldn't have that obnoxiousness to contend with. Were her unsexy breather and her sicko Mr. Clean one and the same? Maybe staring at the tube was in order after all.

Still, as Helena had pointed out, Caroline's car was about the only place she could tolerate disorder for long. Her living quarters was another story. Consequently, it was a contradiction of her nature to leave that wastebasket upended and scraps spilled around.

She was contemplating her compulsiveness and whether the chaos of this visit might be a message to let go a little before fate came along and broke her apart at her rigid places, when she bent down to pick up the wastebasket and replace its contents.

She had retrieved the first scrap and deposited it when she found herself struck still, exactly as she had been in her car when she'd looked into the back seat. This time she was staring at the paper in her hand. She recognized where it came from. She had made some random notes for her breakfast meeting with Mike yesterday morning—points of interest she had jotted down from the files he'd given her. The notes were in no special order, key phrases rather than complete thoughts or sentences. No one but she would have been able to discern their meaning.

The note pages had been on the dresser when she came here to change for dinner at Art's last night. Because it was part of her sense of professional responsibility to be extra careful where papers were concerned, she had taken a moment right then to check through those notes before discarding them. As she finished with each page, having assured herself there was nothing either confidential or decipherable there, she had wadded it up and thrown it into the wastebasket, this same wastebasket she had just knocked over.

At a quick glance none of the pages appeared to be missing. But what *was* apparent was that the pages were no longer wadded up. Someone had smoothed each of them out as flat as could be managed. Even miscellaneous scraps and wrappers had been neatly pressed.

Caroline hurried to the phone, replaced the cord and punched the receiver button several times to get a dial tone. The front desk took longer than usual to answer, and she was impatient by the time she got to ask her question.

"This is Caroline Hardin. Was housekeeping in my room last evening?"

There was a pause on the other end of the line before the operator said, "I'm not quite sure I understand what you're asking."

"I want to know precisely when your staff was in my room to clean yesterday."

"Would you like to speak to the manager? I can have him call you as soon as he comes in."

"This is a very simple question." Caroline could hear the edge in her voice, but for the moment she didn't care. "What time of day do your maids clean the rooms on my corridor? Is that specific enough?"

"Yes, it is, Miss Hardin," the operator said, straining to be polite. "For people not yet checking out, the rooms get cleaned between noon and four. Usually they're done by three."

"Is there any chance the maid could have done my room after five or six last night?"

"No chance at all. They've all gone home by then."

"Thank you."

Caroline hung up the phone. She knew how bizarre that interrogation must have sounded, but she didn't have time for explanations now. She was headed back to the wastebasket when the phone rang. She jumped at the noise, which seemed more janglingly intrusive than ever.

"Oh, no. What if it's the breather again?"

She should have unplugged the phone the minute she got off it. She was tempted to do that now. Instead, she picked it up but didn't say anything.

"Miss Hardin, are you there?" It was the hotel operator again.

"Yes, I'm here. What is it?"

The operator hesitated before asking, "Is everything all right, Miss Hardin? Is there something I can do for you?"

Caroline took a deep breath to calm herself. When she spoke her voice was more evenly modulated. "Everything is just fine," she said. "Thank you for asking."

The operator sounded reluctant to believe that but rung off anyway after repeating that if there was anything Caroline needed, she should call the desk.

Caroline put down the phone and headed back across the room. She scooped up the remaining pages from the floor and retrieved the one she had dropped into the wastebasket earlier. Then she made a beeline for the door before the phone could ring again, forcing her to repeat the gargantuan lie that everything was anywhere near all right.

Caroline barely missed colliding with a four-wheel drive vehicle full of noisy adolescents in her rush to get across the street to the police station. She was further frustrated by Mike's being tied up in a meeting with his assistant, Detective Palumbo. By the time she got into Mike's office, her earlier attempts at controlling her agitation had worn thin. Still, when she saw him, so handsome and rugged-looking with his tie pulled loose, she nearly forgot the sheaf of wrinkled papers in her hand and the reason she had dashed over here to see him.

"Is that something you want to show me," he asked, nodding toward the disheveled pages, "or did you just want to use my trash basket?"

Caroline stood staring at him. His tone was so cool it hit her like an arctic blast and froze her silent. The expression on his face was equally aloof. This behavior was so far out of sync with what they had been to each other last night that she was momentarily disoriented, as if she might have walked into the wrong place by mistake and this wasn't the same man at all who had spoken so tenderly to her only hours ago.

"Caroline? Was there something you wanted?"

He never used her full name. There had to be something wrong. "Are there more problems with the murder cases?"

"No more than usual."

"I see." Caroline sat down in the chair opposite his desk. That frustrations of the investigation might have explained his mood, even the unwarranted sarcasm. "What's been happening," she asked to cover her confusion.

"We've been looking more closely at Parnell Janeway. Reliable sources tell us he's a real nut case, even more than I suspected. This whole investigation is beginning to feel like fright night on the funny farm to me," he growled. Then he looked straight into her eyes with a steely gray gaze. "Was that what you came over here for? To ask me about the investigation? And, if so, what is that stuff in your lap?"

There it was again—the unmistakable chill. Something was definitely wrong. Unfortunately, Caroline hadn't a clue what that might be, and this didn't feel like the right time to ask. She put the sheaf of papers on his desk instead.

"I think this may be the evidence you have been asking for about Justin. You may not see it that way at first, but I hope you'll hear me out before making a judgment."

Caroline was surprised at how calmly she said that. When she came in here she had been anything but calm. But Mike's coolness had subdued her considerably. Meanwhile, Mike looked as if the last thing he cared to do right now was hear anybody out about anything, but he listened anyway. Caroline told him everything that had happened that morning before getting to the heart of what she had concluded from those incidents.

"The night I first got here, when Willow came to my room, she told me about some of the things Justin had done to her. Do you remember my mentioning that to you?"

"Sure. I remember." Mike might be listening, but he didn't sound particularly impressed by what he was hearing.

"Scary phone calls, always letting her know he was watching her and able to get to her whenever he wanted to." Caroline tapped the smoothed out papers for emphasis. "This was what made me put it all together. The calls. Somebody going through my car, even through my trash. Letting me know I'm accessible, vulnerable. Letting me know someone knows where I am when. The things that are happening to me are the same kind of things that Justin did to Willow."

"Allegedly did to Willow," Mike corrected. "There is no concrete evidence that he did anything to anybody. And these scraps of paper aren't evidence, either. They're just scraps of paper."

"Can't you dust them for fingerprints or something?"

Mike thumped back in his chair and laughed, but there was no humor in it. "I have a budget that is watchdogged for every penny. Do you really think I can spend lab time and money on something like this? Besides, if Justin is the diabolical mastermind you seem to think he is, don't you think he'd be clever enough to wear gloves while making criminal entry to your room? Or maybe he'd have one of his henchmen do it. The guys Willow claims he has armies of in his employ."

"You don't have to be sarcastic." Caroline was beginning to feel annoyed, as well as hurt, by his behavior. "I'm just trying to get to the bottom of what's happened to Willow."

Mike lurched forward over his desk in a movement so abrupt it startled Caroline almost as much as the hard, angry expression on his face.

"Maybe what you're really trying to do," he nearly growled, "is still trying to prove something to everybody in this town. Maybe you're even trying to prove that you're not only intelligent, but that you're smarter than all of us put together. You breeze back in here after years of making a big success of yourself, and you favor us with your superor wisdom. While all the time you're looking down your nose because you think you're so much better than we are."

"Mike, what are you talking about?" she gasped, stunned at his unwarranted and unexpected vitriol.

"I'm talking about the way you toy with people, then push them away."

"What do you mean? Wait. Are you talking about people, or about us? And, if you are talking about us, I wouldn't call last night exactly pushing you away."

Mike had lowered his voice to a menacing rumble. "You got what you wanted, then you crept out of the house in the middle of the night. I woke up this morning and you were gone, without so much as a word."

Caroline hardly knew what to say. "I didn't want to wake you," she explained.

"You didn't want to let the light of day shine on the fact that we were lovers. That would make it too real for you. You might just have to face it then as something more than a one-night stand. Isn't that right?"

Caroline opened her mouth, but nothing came out. She wanted to tell him that what he was saying was not true. But perhaps what he was saying was partially true. Yet, she wasn't quite sure what she should or could do about it.

She rose slowly from her chair, picked up the papers from his desk and looked into his angry stare, her own eyes pleading for understanding he couldn't give. Then she turned and left his office, doubting she would ever be able to return.

Chapter Fourteen

Caroline did not go back to her hotel the rest of that morning. She drove all over town, slowly along the streets she had walked as a girl growing up here. Several times she parked the car and walked, gazing at the houses and the old, spreading trees full with summer-green leaves. Finally, she walked the Public Square at the center of town. She examined the display windows and wandered through the shops. She even sat on the bench at the corner where the Woolworth store had been when she was growing up here, the first Woolworth's in the country established by Frank W. Woolworth himself and one of young Caro's favorite places to wander and daydream.

Caroline's odyssey might have appeared to be a meandering one, but she knew exactly where she was going and what she was doing all along the way. She was saying goodbye. She was looking very hard at these streets and street corners—this storefront where she had once lingered after school to gab with girlfriends, that lane through Thompson Park where she had dawdled after swimming at the municipal pool and later first tried her hand at learning to drive.

She stared at each spot as intently as she could, etching every detail in her memory. She knew she was seeing these places for the very last time. When she left Watertown, as she planned to do tomorrow, she would keep the vow she had made all those years ago after high school graduation. She would never return.

She had pledged the same thing once before, years ago, but this was different. She had made that adolescent promise to herself out of anger and resentment, which was bound to abate now and then over the years. Today's promise was made with the sadness of a truth she must resign herself to forever.

She was surprised to find little bitterness left toward this town and its people. The part of herself where that murky cloud had hovered for so long had somehow opened up and released the animosity born of years of having her dreams and aspirations trivialized or dismissed outright. She'd closed her heart all those years ago, deliberately shutting out her unhappy childhood and youth. But she'd returned five days ago, and her heart had been opened once more— by the realization of a girlish fantasy finally come true.

Now that fantasy itself had been dashed against unyielding reality, shattered. But this place wasn't to blame for that. She and Mike had simply missed their time, and now it was too late for them.

She felt that loss deeply, and she knew that sadness would remain with her for a long time to come. What she hadn't expected was this sadness at leaving her home place, her roots, however tortured and twisted they might be. She understood now that this was where she had begun, that her history explained much of what she had become. The roots of the woman she was could be traced straight back to the square of cracked sidewalk pavement where she stood at this moment. Cutting herself off from those roots finally and forever would require a personal history-ectomy that could not be accomplished without pain.

Still, she had to make the break once and for all. She couldn't bear the thought of remaining in the same town with Mike, to be so near and yet so very far from the one man she had ever truly loved.

There. She had finally admitted the truth. The once-simply impossible truth. And it was light-years too late.

Caroline finally returned to the hotel and made her routine stop at the desk for messages. The pink phone-message slip made her heart sink even deeper into despondency. Mike wanted her to come to the police station. He wanted her to observe an interrogation and render an opinion on the subject's psychological state.

How could he ask that of her? Didn't he know how hurt she was? How devastating a wound he had inflicted upon her? Obviously he understood none of that, and Caroline knew why. He didn't understand because he felt no such devastation himself.

Caroline clenched the message into a ball in her fist. He needed her help, and she had made a commitment to do so. But maybe this was more than even Caroline the consummate professional could handle. Maybe this one time she could not live up to what was expected of her.

Meanwhile, she had barely glanced at the other item from her message box. She was mildly surprised at receiving a letter here, and on the way to her room she glanced down at the envelope. Then she stopped dead in her tracks and pulled the letter closer to her face so she could read it more clearly.

There was no mistaking what she saw. The handwriting on this envelope was Willow's.

"I PROCLAIM responsibility for these righteous acts," said Parnell Janeway.

Mike had a special persona he took on for interrogations. He walked through the doorway, eased the door almost shut, then snapped it fast the rest of the way so it closed with a crack that jolted the suspect to attention. Mike would have preferred a metal door that clanged when he slammed it, like the final and terrifying sound of a cell door slamming shut on a criminal's life.

Even before Mike walked through that door he had calculated every move for the purpose of maximum intimidation to set the suspect off balance and make him more vulnerable. Unfortunately, nothing from his bag of tricks and techniques was working with Parnell Janeway this afternoon.

Mike had learned long ago to observe every detail in an interrogation situation—how the suspect sat, the gesture he made, the expression on his face, the inflections of his voice. From those clues, Mike could generally hazard a fair guess at whether or not the subject was telling the truth. These observations wouldn't be admissible in a court of law, but they could often signal Mike when he was pumping a dry hole or maybe even where to drill next. His instincts told him Janeway was dry.

Parnell hadn't been the least bit intimidated by even tough-cop tactics, and Mike guessed that The Preacher didn't feel any of the anxiety most people experience in police custody because he was right where he wanted to be, doing exactly what he wanted to be doing. He was confessing to the riverbank murders and, as he called it, unburdening his immortal soul. However, it was yet to be established whether or not this confession had, in fact, anything to do with the killings.

Mike had to keep his mind clear of judgments right now. Otherwise, he might miss something he'd been predisposed not to hear. He also had to keep himself from thinking about who was watching the video monitor in the next room, able to see every move he made and hear every word he said. Blocking that awareness and the personal turmoil it made him feel had been the real challenge of this interview from the moment it began.

Why had he asked her to come in the first place? He could use her insight, but was it worth the torture of having her so close when he knew she was really worlds away? Whatever the answer, he'd been kicking himself for doing it ever since Palumbo told him she'd arrived and was in the observation room.

Why had she answered his summons, anyway? There was another tough question. Hadn't she made very clear how little he and, therefore his concerns mattered to her? All she cared about was that ditzy friend of hers and getting back to her high-powered life in the big city. So why hadn't she ignored the message he'd left at her hotel in response to an obviously crazy impulse earlier that afternoon? Why was she here?

Maybe that was where the true torture came in. Maybe she was here to watch him do his act, and then she'd do hers, letting everybody know just how smart she was and then packing up and leaving. Mike knew he should be thinking, "Good riddance to her, if that's what she's really like," but his heart wouldn't let him be that cold no matter how hard he tried.

Meanwhile, he had a job to do. He willed his concentration to focus on the man in the chair at the bare wooden table in this fluorescent-lit room. Janeway was slight in stature and pale, with splotches of brown skin discoloration here and there. Those splotches were especially visible on his neck and emphasized by the way he thrust his head forward when making a point, in a gesture that made him resemble a tortoise. He was bald on top with a bordering of straight, sparse gray. His eyes were small and intense when he was impassioned, as was the case at the moment.

Janeway had been born in Canada but raised locally by strict Yankee relatives. He had been a quiet, withdrawn young man and even into his twenties had spent most of his time alone, virtually unnoticed. Then he had taken up what he called his mission, to preach against the corrupt and tainted of the world. His motive might have been religious conversion, as most assumed, or simply the result of a disappointing life marked by unfulfilled expectations and too little excitement.

All Mike knew for certain was that Parnell Janeway was a very angry man who lived on the fringes of society, a fanatic with a volatile personality officially documented in complaints against his street-corner tirades. Consequently, Mike had to disregard his skepticism and consider Parnell a serious suspect, at least for the time being.

He decided to try another interrogation technique—silence. No matter how unintimidated Parnell might be by the prospect of jail and a trial, he was obviously agitated, fired up by the excitement of what was happening and keyed tight with nervous energy. In his present state of mind, he might not be able to let a period of silence go unfilled.

Mike had asked lots of questions—simple, straightforward and calmly put—and Parnell had answered eagerly, thrusting his head forward, gesturing sporadically to emphasize what he was saying. He had talked fast, the words pushing out of him as if thrust into voice by a force that was not to be denied. When one of these verbal eruptions subsided, instead of asking another question, Mike said nothing. Instead, he stared at Janeway, looking directly into his face in complete silence.

Barely a minute passed before Parnell's agitation grew even more pronounced. Soon he was filling the silence with another tumble of words. Mike's bet was that Parnell would eventually say too much.

That finally happened as Parnell described the scenes where the bodies had been found. At first he stuck to the details reported on television and in the papers. Then, perched on the edge of his chair like a large, hyperactive bird in an uncomfortable nest, he succumbed to the lure of the void—silence—and began to put embellishing wings on his story. The flights of fancy he came up with were imaginative, even intriguing, but they bore little resemblance to the truth.

When Mike told Janeway he was released from custody, the man refused to leave. He insisted he'd done the killings in the name of a pure and meaningful cause and that his arrest and trial must go forward to bring this cause to the attention of the nation and the world.

Now Mike knew the motive for Parnell's confession. And when his insistence of guilt got him nowhere, Janeway threatened to go to the press anyway. He would tell everyone his story and all about Mike's incompetence as a police officer, as well. Mike had no doubt Parnell would do just that. He might even capture a headline or two. But Mike couldn't concern himself about that any more than he could waste additional time listening to Parnell carry on.

The sergeant ushered The Preacher out. Mike sank back into a chair and stared at the wall. He was in an alley that could hardly be blinder. And not just because of the way these murder investigations were going. He was up a blind alley with Caro, too.

He didn't really believe all the angry things he'd said or thought about her earlier. Rather, out of frustration with his work and hurt over her obvious willingness to run from what they could have together, he'd gone for her emotional jugular, taking a shred of truth—her need to prove something to a town that had betrayed her—and twisting it like a knife he could hold at her throat. She had shown up in his office at the worst possible time this morning, when leads on his worst case to date had him nearly as tangled up as they were, and he'd lashed out at her in his helpless rage.

Maybe he could explain that to her now and apologize for venting his anger and frustration on her. Maybe she would understand.

"You're really letting these cases get to you." Palumbo was standing in the doorway as Mike pulled his jacket on to leave. "I've never seen you this obsessed before."

Mike shrugged but didn't answer. He didn't want to talk about work right now. He wanted to talk to Caro.

"But then, it's been a long time since I've seen you in a situation where there was a woman in the mix."

Mike wasn't surprised to find his partner so attuned to his feelings. The two of them had worked hand in glove for years. They knew each other better than brothers, the way two men do when one's life can literally depend on the other.

"You're right about that, but I can't get into it just now."

"Then I'll butt myself out," Palumbo said, taking Mike's arm as he was about to brush past out of the room. "Look, Mike, I think I know where you're headed, but Ms. Hardin is gone."

Mike stared at Palumbo. "What do you mean? I asked her to watch the interrogation so I could discuss it with her afterward."

"She said to tell you it was a brilliant job of questioning and that, since you'd nailed Janeway's false confession to the wall in no uncertain terms, there was no reason for her to stick around. So she left."

Mike sighed and shook his head, suddenly aware of just how badly he'd blown it with Caro.

"I don't want to step out of line here," Palumbo was saying, "but can an old married man give you a word of advice?"

"Sure. Why not?"

"I find that explaining myself as clearly as I can manage is the best thing to do whenever me and Margo have problems. As they say, you gotta communicate."

Mike shook his head again. "I tried that once already. Then I screwed up again. I don't think Caro's going to listen to more talk this time. I have to try something else."

"Like what?" Palumbo asked.

CAROLINE DIDN'T OFTEN get depressed. Whenever she felt a bout of the doldrums coming on, she'd make herself even busier than usual till the low point had passed. If she were downstate today, she'd be doing just that.

Unfortunately, she wasn't downstate, and there were no mountains of work to hide behind. She had come here to help Willow, and evidently she'd failed. What she had accomplished was to add new, even more painful wounds to her hometown memory bank.

She had tried to live out a fantasy with the one north country man who had stayed in her heart, and the real-life version had all but destroyed her last happy daydream. She had known highs and lows she hadn't expected to experience here or anywhere. She had known panic and passion. And she had found life-giving warmth in a cold summer.

But all that was over now. There was no longer any doubt what Mike thought of her. He'd made that clear this morning. Oh, he might be attracted to her physically. He might even have come to respect her professionally, at least a little bit.

Gaining that respect had meant everything to her. That was why she'd gone to the interrogation this afternoon, even though she knew how much it would hurt to see him again. Mike hadn't been there to meet her when she arrived at the station; he'd assigned Detective Palumbo that duty. Then there he was on the video screen, cool and calm, manipulating the suspect perfectly at every turn. If Mike had anything besides his job on his mind, all of Caroline's powers of observation couldn't detect it.

Unfortunately, she hadn't been able to be quite so single-minded. Whatever she might have achieved in her life—her academic accomplishments and professional successes—felt suddenly hollow, devoid of the satisfaction they had once given her. She loved Mike Schaeffer, and that was all that mattered. Clearly, though, he didn't love her. Judging by what he'd said this morning, he didn't even like her very much.

That awareness lay like a weight on her heart. She could hardly move about her hotel room for the burden of it.

It was enough to make Caroline feel a bit abused by life at the moment. She hardly needed the additional blow this day had dealt her; when she learned she'd been made a fool of by her best friend. The letter Caroline picked up at the hotel desk earlier that afternoon revealed that Willow had lied. Everything Caroline had done these past days, supposedly on Willow's behalf, had been based on a falsehood. Willow had tricked Caroline into coming to the north country and had been tricking her ever since.

According to Willow's letter written in the feathery hand that was so unmistakably hers, she had exaggerated her situation with Justin for the purpose of gaining Caroline's sympathy and help, but a belated attack of conscience had stopped her from using her friend, and she'd taken off on her own instead. She was most apologetic, in her northern belle way of phrasing it, for having dragged Caroline up here under false pretenses. Willow went on to lament any damage she might have caused their friendship and pleaded for understanding.

Caroline might have been more open to that plea if it hadn't been for the toll this trip had taken on her emotions. If Willow hadn't lured her home, Mike Schaeffer would have remained a distant romantic memory. She'd have been spared the very unromantic grief she was feeling now.

After her excruciating hour of watching Mike on that video monitor, she had thought of leaving a note with Detective Palumbo to tell Mike that Willow was safe. But she'd decided she could do that more easily and cleanly on her way out of town. Now she was choosing the perhaps psychologically unenlightened but easiest way to beat her emotional exhaustion. She decided to sleep it off before beginning her trek back to Westchester.

Caroline stripped to her underwear and sought the womblike comfort of the bed. She mounted pillows around her in the closest thing to a nest she could manage. She had left the entryway light on to create a soft glow against the darkness imposed by the blackout curtains even at this hour of the afternoon. She settled herself into this soothing niche and was drifting away from consciousness when the realization struck.

She sat bolt upright, disordering the cocoon of bedding. There was something about Willow's letter, something that suddenly did not ring true. Caroline leapt out of bed and darted to the dresser, where she had left the envelope and single page of monogrammed stationary. She flipped on the dresser lamp and leaned toward it to make out the words Willow had written.

Caroline had read the letter only once through after opening it. She'd done so with increasing discouragement as she progressed from line to line. Consequently, she hadn't been as attentive to the later sections of the message as to Willow's opening revelation of what she'd done. It was there, in the last paragraph, that the troubling sentence appeared, after Willow's appeal to Caroline to be understanding.

"And I implore you not to tell Della of my shameful behavior," Willow wrote in her characteristic antique way. "I am absolutely certain she would never forgive me."

There was the false note, ringing loud and clear, as perhaps only Caroline could hear it. For Caroline knew that there was nothing Willow could ever do that Della wouldn't forgive her for. She loved her daughter deeply and unconditionally exactly as she was, and Willow knew that, too. It was the quality of their relationship Caroline had envied most, and Willow had agreed that such parental regard was truly a blessing in life.

The last thing Willow might concern herself with, in this or any other crisis, would be the possibility of losing her mother's love or understanding. That wasn't what she actually meant in this note at all. She was sending Caroline a message, in as subtle terms as possible. All was not well or as it seemed, especially with what Willow had written in the rest of the letter.

Because of its subtlety, no one but Caroline would be likely to recognize that one sentence as a clue to Willow's true situation. Mike would certainly think Caroline was exaggerating the significance here. Only Della Gilchrist would know Caroline was right, and she wasn't about to worry that dear lady with the frightening implications of this message.

One of those implications was that, if Willow had had to disguise her call for help so cleverly, she must have considered herself in real danger of discovery when she wrote this. She must have feared what might happen to her if an underlying message should be detected. Caroline was convinced more strongly than ever that her friend was in jeopardy, and that the person frightening her so badly was none other than the man who "feared" she might never return. Her husband, Justin Fowler.

MIKE HADN'T CALLED Justin's office to announce this visit. Better to catch him off guard, just in case he really did have something to hide. Ever since Caroline had left Mike's office this morning, the voice of hunch had been telling him that there might be something to her suspicions. Maybe there were too many loose ends here after all. Willow was gone, and she hadn't been in touch with anyone since she left. Whether this was a pattern for her or not, no evidence had come to light to prove she was following that pattern now. Also, the journal could be exactly what Caroline surmised, a collection of Willow's private fantasies. Recalling its wording, Mike could see the credibility of that interpretation.

Furthermore, Nate Conklin might be in love with Willow, but he was hardly the kind of guy who gave way to hysteria. Yet he'd called Mike this afternoon sounding almost hysterical. He said he'd hesitated to be in touch before now because that might get Willow into even more trouble with Justin, and Nate was concerned about what Justin might do to her. Unfortunately, Nate said, after such a long silence from his friend, he believed Willow could already be in that kind of trouble with Justin, and, therefore, in need of help.

Finally, there were Caroline's fears that Willow might have been kidnapped, or worse. In these past few days, Mike had learned to respect Caroline as a clear thinker and competent professional. She worked in a business similar to his own, observing, listening, picking up clues to what was really going on underneath the surface of the way things appeared to be. Making connections, intuitive and otherwise.

Caroline had put together the pieces of what was happening to her—obnoxious phone calls, somebody messing around in her car and her hotel room—and made a connection to some things Willow had told her. So maybe he should be paying attention to those conclusions rather than dismissing them out of hand. Maybe if he hadn't been so preoccupied with the riverbank murders, he would have given her that attention sooner.

Well, better late than never. Before taking off to see Justin, Mike had set Palumbo to work checking out Fowler's background, especially for any discrepancies from the vague generalities he'd let be known about his personal history. Palumbo assured Mike this was an assignment he would relish, since he'd never cottoned to the high-powered financial consultant in the first place. Palumbo would leave no computer chip unturned until he'd found out everything there was to know about the man.

Meanwhile, Mike had driven up Washington Street and walked, unexpected, into Justin's office in the hope of maybe catching him off guard at least for a moment. The fact that Mike wasn't in the habit of making such visits and that this one came so close on the heels of his being here with Caroline could possibly do the trick.

Now Justin greeted Mike with his usual big smile. To any other than the finely attuned eye, he would have seemed totally at ease. Mike, however, had his observation skills at high pitch. He thought he detected, though only barely, the flicker of anxiety beneath the joviality of Justin's welcome.

"Schaeffer. What a pleasant surprise." Justin clasped Mike's hand as he entered the plush but casual office.

Mike let Justin take a seat on one of the deep-cushioned sofas but remained standing.

"Make yourself comfortable," Justin said, gesturing to the other couch. "Keeping the peace must be tiring, especially these days."

"Actually, it's got me pretty charged up," Mike said. "I feel more like pacing than sitting right now, thanks."

He turned on his heel and walked across the room to Justin's desk, then around to the back of it. Mike bent forward for a moment, examining what he saw on the desktop. He let his glance linger on the appointment calendar with deliberate obviousness. He strolled out from behind the desk and over to a small bookcase, turning his back on Justin supposedly to peruse the titles.

"This situation with your wife has been bothering me, Justin. Maybe you could shed some light on the questions I can't seem to stop asking myself about it."

"What questions are those?"

Mike turned around slowly and clasped his hands behind him. He rocked backward on his heels to assume his most effective authoritarian pose.

"You seem so completely convinced that nothing could have happened to her," he said. "I know that if my wife took off in the middle of the night without a word, I'd be imagining all kinds of nightmare possibilities, even if she had a history of taking off in the past. I think most men would feel the same. How is it that you're so calm about the whole thing?"

Justin stared back at him for a moment. Mike could tell nothing from Justin's eyes, other than that he appeared to be making a decision of some kind. Then the man looked down at his clasped hands and sighed.

"I hadn't wanted to tell you this, Mike," Justin began. "I was hoping I could put off the humiliation for a while longer. But I guess that isn't going to be possible."

"What humiliation is that?"

Mike maintained his distance and his interrogative posture. Justin had to look up at him when he finally did raise his head, and the expression on his face was either sincerely stricken or a well-executed approximation.

"I believe my wife left me for another man, and that I gave her the money to do it."

"When did you give her money? Caroline said Willow didn't have much with her that evening they met."

"I saw Willow one last time after she talked to Caroline."

Mike gave no outward sign that he was surprised by that revelation. He just waited and listened, as he had with Parnell Janeway. A low-key approach might also work with a high-energy character like Fowler.

"She asked me for money," Justin went on, "just like she always did."

Mike ignored this obvious put-down of Willow. "How did she get in touch with you?"

"She called me."

"Is that so?"

"Yes, it is."

Mike moved at last. He kept his hands clasped behind his back and appeared to be pondering the thick carpet as he walked slowly to the couch Justin had previously indicated. Perhaps this easy, relaxed pace would be maddening for a kinetic personality like Justin. Mike unclasped his hands, hitched up his trouser legs for comfort and took his time sitting down. To turn the tension up yet another notch, he gave Justin a tight, enigmatic smile before speaking again.

"Where exactly did Willow call you from?" he asked.

"I don't know." Did Justin sound a shade less in control? "She refused to tell me."

"Did she come back to your house to get the money?"

"No. She said she didn't want to do that."

"I see." Mike rubbed his toe back and forth a couple of times in the heavy carpet nap and bobbed his head thoughtfully for a moment. "So you went to meet her?"

"Yes, that's right."

"Whose idea was it where you should meet? Yours or hers?"

"Whose idea was it?"

Justin appeared to be confused, but Mike had seen this kind of stumbling act before when the subject was trying to figure out how best to avoid incriminating himself. Mike didn't make it any easier on Justin by rephrasing the question. He simply waited for Justin to fill in the silence that now yawned between them.

"I guess it was her idea," he said finally.

"And where did Willow have you meet her?"

"She insisted on somewhere outside of town."

"Could that have been on the road to Burrville?"

Justin was brushing a piece of invisible lint from his trousers, and at that question his hand halted over his lap, the fingers curved as if they had forgotten their mission. It occurred to Mike that this was the first time he'd ever seen Justin obviously taken by surprise.

"No," he said, maybe too adamantly. "We didn't meet there."

Mike wouldn't press him further for the location just yet. "So you met her and gave her money?"

"Yes, I did."

"How much did you give her?"

"A thousand dollars."

Mike whistled low. "That's quite a piece of change."

"Willow never asked for small amounts. She's an expensive lady." Justin appeared to relax a bit, maybe because he'd been given the opportunity to score another hit against Willow's moral character.

"How did that work, giving her the money and all?" Mike asked.

"What do you mean, how did it work? I don't understand what you're asking."

"Did Willow ask you for the money when she called you? Did she tell you the amount she wanted? Did you have that much cash just lying around?"

Justin's ingratiating smile narrowed to a thin line. "Yes, she asked me for money when she called. Yes, she told me how much to bring. No, I didn't have that much 'lying around,' but I did have it in my safe at home."

"Let me get this straight now. Your wife called you up late at night demanding that you meet her somewhere on the outskirts of town with a thousand dollars cash. And you went ahead and did just that, even though you suspected she would use it to leave with another man?"

"I didn't begin to think there might be another man involved until after she had gone."

"Even so, you certainly were a generous and understanding husband to go along with her demands that way."

Justin nodded sadly and clasped his hands in his lap. "I think that may have been my big mistake with Willow from the start. I've been *too* generous and understanding."

"Why didn't you tell me this when I questioned you about it before?"

"Come on, Mike. You should be able to figure that one out. You live in this town. You know how hard it is to keep a story like this quiet. And you know how the tongues are going to wag once it gets out."

Mike nodded. Tongues were going to wag all right. But would they be spreading the tale Justin had just told him, or another version of what had happened to Willow Fowler?

Chapter Fifteen

Caroline might have read every Nancy Drew mystery in the library when she was a girl, but that didn't make her any more comfortable with sneaking around behind the scenes after a bad guy. Still, she was more certain than ever that Willow was in need of rescuing, and Willow had come through as Caroline's friend in need too many times in the past to let her down now.

But what, exactly, was she to do?

She had stayed in her room all last evening pondering that very question. The turkey club sandwich she had ordered from room service still sat, barely touched, on the table near the window this morning. She'd been too preoccupied to think about food last night, and this morning she was too agitated to be hungry. Maybe she would lose those few extra pounds that she and just about every other woman she knew were forever intent upon shedding. That might be one good thing to come out of this nerve-racking situation. But nothing would be any good unless she was able to help Willow out of whatever peril she was in.

A burst of determination to do just that got Caroline moving. She still hoped that all of this was only a case of too much melodramatic imagination. She would much prefer to discover that Willow had been in no real trouble all along and that eagerness to make up for all she owed Willow from their growing up years had prompted Caroline to imagine a threat to her friend where there actually was none.

Then her glance fell on Willow's note where it lay on the dresser top. Caroline didn't need to read the words again to know with every instinct she had that she had not been exaggerating Willow's circumstances. Her friend needed help, and she needed it now.

Caroline dressed for a day of action in jeans, sneakers, sweatshirt and jacket, the one down-to-earth outfit among the designer numbers she'd carried up here. She smiled without amusement at her earlier notion of dressing to impress. Today she hoped she was truly dressing for success.

She thought of the success that would forever elude her now—knowing Mike's love. Images leapt into her head before she could stop them, and feelings, too. She didn't want to remember his arms around her, his hands touching her body and soul. Welcome or not, sensation engulfed her as his arms once had, threatening to overwhelm her with sweet bitterness. She could not deny these feelings and their power over her. She could only hope to leave them behind here in her solitary room, while she put into motion her current action.

CAROLINE HAD A TELEPHONE in her hotel room—no doubt about that—but she needed a pay phone for what she had to do this morning. And a particular pay phone at that. She also had to wait until she was certain Justin would be in his office. She didn't want Martha sidetracking this call. Willow had mentioned in the past that Justin was so compulsive about his work that he made a habit of getting to his office even before the rest of the staff arrived in the morning.

"He probably wants to read their calendars and go through their desk drawers," Caroline muttered to herself as she turned the key in the ignition and the car roared to life.

Her dark humor hit a chord. Justin could very well be an obsessive-compulsive personality . . . as she had described in her profile for Mike. There was no telling what more he might do to keep everyone in his personal sphere, including Willow, securely under his thumb. And if he could no longer control his wife . . .

Caroline understood that she was about to challenge Justin's sense of control perhaps more blatantly than anyone ever had, at least since childhood, when somebody, most likely one or both of his parents, had done the damage to Justin's ego to make him what he was today. If Caroline's thumbnail analysis was correct, he would consider that challenge an unbeatable threat, and he could react strongly, even violently.

There was no way of guessing, even approximately, what he might do if she tripped the switch that pushed him beyond the array of emotional checks and balances that maintained his self-control, those safeguards that kept him smiling on the surface and always intent upon doing precisely the right thing. Once past their boundaries, he could turn into a loose cannon of unpredictable force and velocity, perhaps blasting off straight at her.

She reminded herself that, whatever the risk, she had to go forward with her plan and follow up closely—very closely—on the results. Willow's safety could depend on it. Thus the very particular pay phone.

As she turned onto Washington Street, she cast a last longing glance at the municipal building across the corner. She was afraid, more afraid than she had ever been, and she wished Mike, or even Detective Palumbo, could come along with her for this morning ride. But she could just hear how the two of them would scoff at her concern over one sentence in what looked like a casual scribbled note from Willow. Then, when they heard the scheme Caroline had dreamed up to capture the villain in his own net, they'd be hard-pressed to keep from laughing right in her face.

Caroline's foot hit the accelerator with added resolve. There'd be no assistance forthcoming from the municipal building. In fact, there would be no help from any quarter at all. She was on her own in this, and she knew it. No time to worry about that now. Only time to act...and to pray that this was her—and Willow's—lucky day.

The pay phone on the corner across from Justin's building provided the perfect location. Except for one scary possibility. Thinking about that possibility made her heart skip inside her throat.

If Justin happened to look out one of the front windows of his second-floor office, he might see her on the opposite corner. That could be disastrous, both for herself and Willow. Still, Caroline had to take the chance. It was a calculated risk. The desk where he would most likely take a call did not face the front windows. Of course, he could pick up another phone and glance through the modish, thin-slatted vertical window blinds, and there she would be.

Caroline had no choice. If she was right in her assessment of Justin's psychology, what she was about to do could prompt him to immediate action. She had to be on the spot to observe what that action might be and to follow him in his pursuit of it. She took whatever precautions were possible. She parked her conspicuous yellow car up the block, out of range of Justin's windows. She also grabbed her Mets cap out of the trunk and put it on, tucking her hair inside and pulling the visor down to shadow her face.

Actually a cap was entirely appropriate this morning. The temperature was even more chilling than it had been thus far this cold summer week in the north country. The sky was a lowering gray, and rain was predicted. That could put a literal damper on this mission of hers.

Thinking of this morning's venture in those terms warned Caroline that she might be about to make a colossal fool of herself. If her suspicions proved unfounded, she could come out of this looking like an overly emotional female who wasn't to be taken seriously. She'd worked very hard for a lot of years to avoid exactly that image. Was she about to undo those efforts, in the very critical eyes of her hometown?

Well, however important being seen as a serious professional might be to her, actually being a caring person was far more important. She pulled up the collar of her jacket and hurried toward the phone near the corner.

Too bad phone booths had gone out of style, she thought to herself as she dialed the number of Justin's office. She would have felt less vulnerable behind a closed door, even a glass one. Instead, all she could do was hunch into her jacket, turn her back to the building across the street and say yet another prayer for the chips to fall her way this morning.

The phone rang three times, and Caroline was beginning to wonder if Justin might have changed his pattern and not come in early. Then someone picked up the receiver on the other end of the line, and a voice said, "Hello."

It was definitely Justin. Caroline's heart jumped into her mouth.

"Hello, Justin. This is Caroline Hardin," she managed to say with a semblance of calm.

"Caroline. How good to hear from you on this not so lovely morning."

Oh, no, she thought. He's looking out the window at the weather!

Caroline suppressed the urge to peek behind her to see where he might be doing that looking from. She had never planned to hide her identity as the person making this call, but it was essential to her plan that he not know how close at hand she was to him right now.

"What I have to talk to you about isn't so lovely, either," she said.

"Really? What could that be?"

Caroline heard the cautious tone in his voice. She had him on guard already. Good.

"I woke up this morning to find a letter pushed under the door here in my hotel room." She hoped that hint concerning her supposed whereabouts wouldn't go unnoted. "It was from Willow and postmarked New York City. One of the hotel employees must have delivered it while I was asleep."

"What could possibly be unlovely about that? You were so worried about Willow, and it turns out she's in New York. I would think you'd be very much relieved." There was an edge of annoyance in Justin's voice, along with the caution.

"Except that I'm fairly certain this letter was not actually mailed by Willow, at least not of her own free will. And I don't believe she was in New York City when she wrote it."

"Whatever are you talking about?"

He was obviously trying to affect a scoffing tone, but Caroline thought she detected something else, as well. Could it be fear? Anger? Of course, she was making a wild assumption about the postmark being a ruse, but it seemed possible. At this point, almost anything did.

"I'm talking about what you might call a private code between Willow and me. Remember, we've been close friends for many years. We have a kind of shorthand between us that nobody else would ever be able to detect. I believe Willow was using that shorthand in this note."

"And what was she telling you in this 'shorthand' of yours, as you call it."

His attempt at derision was even more thinly disguised now. Her plan to push him to the edge of his usual control mechanisms seemed to be working.

"I am almost positive," she said. "That Willow is telling me that she is in danger and needs help."

"This is sounding more farfetched by the minute. Do you really expect me—or anyone else, for that matter—to believe any of this?"

"I think she's telling me something else, too," Caroline went on. "I think she's telling me where she is, or at least where she was when she was forced to write this note."

There wasn't much of a pause before Justin responded to that, only a beat or two, but Caroline heard it.

"I'll tell you what I think," he said in a tone as cold as the morning. "I think you need to avail yourself of the services of that clinic of yours. In other words, you're sounding seriously delusional."

"That may be or may not be true, Justin. I have to make one more phone call to be absolutely sure my thinking is correct on this. Meanwhile, I'm of the firm opinion that Willow was sending me a very specific message between the lines of this note." She paused before delivering the final blow. "And I believe her message has a lot to do with you."

"And I am of the firm opinion that you are very far off base."

Off base? For an instant, Caroline had the crazy notion that he was looking out the window, referring to her Mets cap. This time she couldn't resist. She stole a glance over her shoulder at the restored Victorian across the street.

She almost sighed out loud with relief. No one was standing at a window.

"As I said, Justin. One more call and I'll know exactly who is off base and who isn't."

"Who are you going to call and bother about this? Della? You'd better not be calling up that poor old woman and frightening her with crazy stories. She has enough to worry about where Willow is concerned. And if you decide to add to that worry, so help me, you'll be sorry you did."

He had said all that in what sounded like a single breath. Caroline could almost hear the threads of his self-control stretch toward the breaking point. She was all but certain that one more turn of the screw could do the trick.

"You can threaten me all you want, Justin," she said with deliberate calm. "I know what I intend to do, and then you can expect to be hearing from me again. Very soon."

Caroline hung up the phone before he could sputter an irate reply. And sputter was she strongly suspected he would do. She was sure she had him on the run, and that meant she had better do some hustling herself. She hurried back up the block to one of the big old trees that lined the avenue and hid herself behind it. From here, she could see Justin's building, but he wouldn't be able to see her—if and when he did what she was all but certain he was about to do.

MIKE GENERALLY let Palumbo take computer duty. It wasn't that Mike couldn't operate the thing. He simply tended to be too restless and impatient to be well suited to that particular work. When he wanted information, he wanted it yesterday or last week. He didn't feel like sitting in front of a screen, referencing and cross-referencing. So, Palumbo did the deed in that department and liked it, too. He loved the game element of things. To him, working the computer was a trip to the video parlor done in words rather than blasting tanks and aircraft.

Palumbo had been at work on their John Doe already when Mike asked him to check out Fowler, as well. Palumbo had labored over both of those pursuits long into the night. In fact, he'd been at the monitor till nearly dawn. With only a greasy doughnut and innumerable cups of coffee to fortify him against a sleepless night and a new day, he might have been a bit giddy to begin with when the data he'd been looking for finally came through for both searches at about the same time.

When he dashed into Mike's office with the shocking results—and moving that fast wasn't a thing a man Palumbo's size did on a regular basis—he was out of breath and so elated his eyes were shining.

Mike's first thought was that his detective had stayed too long in a local tavern last night and was at the mercy of a hangover this morning. Then the printouts were plopped down on his desk, and he began to share Palumbo's thrill of discovery. For a moment or two.

"Holy sh— Are you absolutely sure there's no mistake here?" Mike asked, glancing in amazement from one sheet to the next.

"I double-checked by phone after it came in."

Palumbo was the restless one now, actually bouncing on the balls of his feet in front of the desk, too excited to confine himself to a chair.

"I always smelled a rat about that guy," he crowed. "But I have to admit, I never would have guessed in a million years it was this big a one."

Mike sighed, his euphoria sobered by reality. "We're going to have to bring him in for questioning and that's going to blow off a lot of lids around here. That could have its downside, you know." Mike was still stunned, trying to figure out how adding two and two had never come out quite this way before.

"I know."

"Ah, hell. It's a dirty job, but someone's got to do it, as the saying goes. Are you feeling up to coming along?"

"I wouldn't miss it for the world."

"I didn't think so."

Mike had put on his jacket as they talked and checked his pocket for his shield. He always did that before a potential arrest. He'd had a dream once where he'd shown up for a big bust without his badge and they wouldn't let him in. That wouldn't happen now, though part of him wished something could postpone this particular rough duty. He was cop first, and cops want criminals off the street, especially in cases like this one. Still, he would have been happy if the computer screen had turned up something less disturbing.

"I want to take along a couple of backups," he was saying as he preceded Palumbo through the office door.

The printouts had been left behind on Mike's desk, with the pertinent references circled in red. One red circle revealed that the name of the first riverbank murder victim, the one probably killed in the building behind the Carriage House Hotel, was George Aloysius Bennett and that he came from Boston. Another red circle on a separate printout revealed that Justin Fowler also hailed originally from Boston.

Mother's name, Grace Fowler. Father's name, George Aloysius Bennett.

CAROLINE FOLLOWED Justin from his office to the house on Flower Avenue West. She kept far behind so the yellow car wouldn't be as conspicuous, while scolding herself for not thinking to get a less identifiable rental. Luckily, Justin appeared too intent on the business at hand to notice her trailing him. When he signaled a turn off Washington Street, she guessed where he was headed.

She parked in a driveway past the Fowler house and left her motor running. Several minutes passed. Then she saw him run back out of the house and head for the three-stall garage. Apparently he wasn't taking the big sedan. A four-wheel-drive vehicle rolled out of the garage instead. Luckily for her, he turned onto the street in the opposite direction from her hiding place.

Caroline waited until he was a block ahead of her before following. A misty rain had begun, and she was glad of that. Visibility out of Justin's rear window would be less sharp now, especially on such a gray morning. What was nagging at her, however, was the fact that he had taken the four-wheel drive. This sports job of hers was hardly an all-terrain vehicle. Justin had better not lead her too far off the beaten track.

MIKE BELIEVED in loyalty, and Justin had tried to be his friend. That loyal part of Mike didn't enjoy heading a parade of police cars to Justin's house, but the man wasn't at his office, so there'd been no other choice. Martha was out of the side door to meet them before the engines had died.

"What in heaven's name is all this about?" she asked.

"We need to speak with Justin," Mike said.

"He isn't here." She had her hands on her hips and stood blocking the doorway behind her.

"We'll have to check on that, Martha," Mike said, gesturing for Palumbo and two of the officers to go inside and search the house.

"You can't do that," Martha nearly shouted as she backed against the screened porch door.

Mike took her arm. "Yes, we can, Martha. We are here on official police business, and I know you wouldn't want to be guilty of obstructing justice."

He let that sink in for a moment before pulling her gently but forcefully away from the door. She didn't resist, but she didn't stop frowning, either.

"I need you to tell me where Mr. Fowler has gone," Mike said.

"I got no idea. He doesn't tell me his comings and goings." The set of Martha's jaw told Mike she was not yet ready to cooperate.

Palumbo came back out of the door behind Martha and shook his head at Mike. Justin wasn't in the house. That meant Mike had to find out what Martha knew, and he had to do so right now.

"Martha, I have to know anything you can tell me about the last time you saw Mr. Fowler, and anything you can tell me about where you think he may have gone."

"I already said he didn't tell me."

"Martha, I understand loyalty, but sometimes other things are more important. This is one of those times," Mike said, deciding whether or not to throw in his ace in the hole. In the end, he had to. "You can either answer my questions here, or I'll have to take you down to the police station for questioning."

"You'd arrest me?"

"Something like that, yes."

Martha's north country facade still didn't crack, except for her eyes, where Mike could see hints of the struggle that was going on inside her. He was banking on her north country pride, as well. She'd know how the gossips would have at her for being arrested. He was positive she'd never been beyond the front desk of a police station, much less interrogated there. Nonetheless, her struggle took a couple of long minutes before his strategy paid off.

"I'm tellin' the truth about him not saying where he was goin', but he took the Bronco."

"Does that mean anything special to you?"

Palumbo had jumped in with that question. Martha gave him a look that could freeze alcohol, and Mike was afraid for a moment that she would clam up again.

But Martha finally did answer, directing what she had to say to Mike while pointedly ignoring Palumbo. "Mr. Fowler bought the Bronco for just one thing. Going out to his hunting camp up near Adams Center."

"I know where it is," Mike said. "Thank you, Martha. I understand that this hasn't been easy for you."

Maybe it was that acknowledgment of the struggle she'd experienced that made her grab Mike's arm as he turned to leave. "One more thing," Martha said.

"You know that young woman you were here with the other day, the one that's a friend of Mrs. Fowler's?"

"Caroline Hardin. What about her?"

A chill of foreboding cut through the one already causing discomfort from the worsening rainfall.

"Well, I watched Mr. Fowler go out of the driveway. I was standing there a minute afterward, trying to figure out why he might be goin' off huntin' on a day like this—and out of season, too—when I saw that yellow car of hers. I think she was following Mr. Fowler."

"Are you sure it was her?"

"Sure as shootin'."

Mike didn't wait to find out more. He practically ran to his car, leaving Palumbo in his wake. Palumbo called out and waved to get Mike's attention, but he didn't stop as he whipped the unmarked car into a U-turn through one of Justin's carefully tended flower beds and tore out of the driveway into the street.

Chapter Sixteen

Caroline's worst fears about Justin taking the four-wheel-drive vehicle had come true with a vengeance, and the rain made it even worse. She had no trouble staying far back while still keeping track of him on the flat, fairly straight highway to Adams Center. Even when he turned off onto a narrower secondary road, high-crowned down the middle from decades of piling new blacktop on old, she could keep out of sight because of the frequent turns and twists. Fortunately, when he took his final turn on a dirt track into the woods, it was from a straight stretch, and she could see exactly where he'd gone. But then her real troubles began.

The rain, which was coming down much harder now, had already begun to make mud of the the two tire trails into the trees, and those trails were too wide for a sports car anyway. She made it to the tree line, bumping along and being lurched against her seat belt. But when she veered off the track to avoid a particularly nasty bounce, her tires hit a boggy spot and began to spin, and that was it. She tried rocking the car forward and back, but that only settled the tires deeper into the rapidly softening earth. Besides, gunning a sports car back and forth was a noisy business. She was afraid Justin might hear her. She had no choice but to get out and walk.

She was grateful for her sneakers and for the tree cover above her. The rain was pounding down now, but once she was into the woods, the leafy branches formed a protective canopy. The raindrops drummed loudly against it, but few got through.

She wondered how far Justin intended to go into the woods and if she would be able to catch him on foot, especially since she could no longer hear his car. Her heart was sinking at the realization that she had very possibly lost him, along with any hope of helping Willow, when it happened.

He burst out of the woods behind her, and he had a hunting rifle. Before she could even cry out, he had the barrel jabbed into her side.

"Not a very good day for a walk in the woods," Justin snarled.

Caroline would have heard the sneer in his voice even if she hadn't seen it on his face. Absurd as it was, all she could think of was Little Red Riding Hood, and she tried to remember what had happened to her.

"That fancy yellow car of yours got you into trouble again, didn't it," he said, prodding her with the barrel to get her walking. "That car has been your downfall, you know, ever since that first night. I knew you saw me, probably even watched me carry the old man out and stuff him in my trunk. Then you thought you'd fool me by not saying anything, put that cop friend of yours on my tail instead. Hah! Just because of you, all of my hard work and planning were for nothing. Chasing down those other two, figuring out where to leave them so they'd get found, dragging them there—all a waste because of you."

Oh, no. Was he talking about what she thought he was talking about? In a way Caroline welcomed his babbling, because it gave her time to think about what to do next. Still, she couldn't tamp down her horror at what she was hearing.

"I have no idea what you're referring to, Justin," she said, doing her best to sound cool and easy, hoping to calm him down. She might have wanted him agitated before, but now he was holding a gun.

"You're just like him." He nudged her with the gun barrel to emphasize his point. "You show up here and ruin everything I've worked so hard for. Then all that comes out of your mouth is lies. You're going to get what he got, too. But, instead of leaving you on the riverbank, I think I'll throw you in and watch you float away."

His ravings were making horrible sense, and even as Caroline's mind rebelled against understanding, she knew her absolute fears were coming true.

EVEN WITHOUT a siren and flashers, Mike had left Palumbo and the others well behind in his frenzied race. Besides, he knew precisely where he was going, and his fellow cops didn't. Justin had hosted the Young Turks at his cabin last hunting season, hoping for one of those real-men-in-the-woods gatherings, and Mike had halfheartedly gone along.

The bad news was that today the tracks in were muddy and treacherous, and maneuvering the sedan was painfully slow going. Mike was feeling increasingly desperate. Then he saw a flash of yellow through the trees.

WILLOW WAS WEARING the same cream-colored silk dress she'd had on the last time Caroline saw her, but now it was minus the jacket, smudged with dirt and torn in places. Willow herself looked even worse. She had obviously been drugged, and though the effects appeared to be wearing off, she was still groggy.

"Willow, are you all right?" Caroline hurried to the plaid couch where Willow was trying to sit up, though she was bound hand and foot.

"I think so," she whispered, her voice hoarse. "But these ropes are hurting me."

Caroline turned on Justin with a sudden fury, despite his upraised rifle. "You untie her this minute!" she shouted over the slap of rain against the cabin roof.

He laughed and made an ugly, mocking face. "Listen to you, giving orders! I'll untie her all right, but not because you say so." He pulled a hunting knife from a sheath on his belt and walked over to Willow, who shrank back at the sight of the blade. "I don't want to have to carry either of you out into the woods to do what I intend to do with you. I've had to drag enough bodies around already."

He was still holding the rifle and keeping an eye on Caroline, but he had to turn for an instant to cut Willow's bonds with two slices of the sharp knife. Ordinarily, if Caroline had found herself at the mercy of a crazed multiple murderer armed with a rifle and a knife, she suspected she would have forced herself to remain icy calm and tried to talk him down.

However, her fury was too hot for that now—and getting hotter by the second. And that rage gave her the courage to act. She lunged and half heard herself utter a sound that was part scream, part growl. She kicked with all the force of her anger, hard and right on target between Justin's thighs.

She wished she'd worn boots instead of sneakers, but the blow did its work anyway. Justin fell to the floor with a thud and a howl, and a wild discharge from the rifle. Caroline didn't wait for another, better-aimed shot. She grabbed Willow's hand and ran for the door.

The rain pounded against them in the clearing outside. Willow's thin silk dress was almost instantly drenched and clung, tangled around her legs. Her feet were bare, and she kept stumbling. Caroline pulled her along, praying the cold rain would snap her out of what was left of her drugged stupor. Justin was only temporarily out of commission. Soon he would be after them.

They were on the dirt track headed back toward Caroline's car when they heard the motorcycle engine. "Oh, no!" Willow gasped trying to pull herself together and run faster.

Caroline stole a glance over her shoulder and saw the big Harley bearing down on them. She hauled on Willow's arm and, to her horror, felt her friend stumble.

Caroline glanced back again in desperation, and at first she didn't comprehend what she saw. Something leapt out of the woods next to the trail and struck bike and biker like a cannon shot, sending Justin sprawling as the bike veered off and slammed into a tree.

"It's . . . Michael . . . Schaeffer," said Willow between gulps for breath.

"Mike!" Caroline cried, dropping Willow's arm and running toward the two men grappling on the ground.

Justin was on top and appeared to have the upper hand. The bike had grazed Mike and he was obviously hurt. Justin was taking full advantage of that. Caroline had just thrown herself onto his back and begun pounding him with her fists when Willow yanked her off.

Fear, cold rain and adrenaline had obviously jolted Willow to full consciousness, and she was now moving fast and deliberately. Caroline didn't see the large round rock in Willow's hands until she had raised it to full arm's height above her head. She brought it down—and struck her husband just above the back of his neck.

Justin froze for an instant, then slumped to the ground at Willow's feet. And in the next instant Caroline was cradling Mike in her arms.

THE YOUNG TURKS MET again the next month as usual, but that was all that was usual about the dinner gathering. The men brought their wives or women friends this time.

Everyone was glad to see Tim Manders in attendance with the former. It seemed that he had been on the wrong side of town that fateful morning the month before because of some extramarital activity there. According to the latest gossip on the subject, however, Tim was securely back in the family fold these days.

Joe Palumbo and his wife, Margo, were also present, at the head table next to Mike. Even more pleasing to Mike was the occupant of the seat on his other side.

Caroline was deep in conversation with Willow Gilchrist and Nate Conklin about the family therapy clinic Caroline was planning to organize in Watertown. Della Gilchrist leaned forward from across the table to hear Caroline above the talk and laughter.

Caroline was obviously inspired by her subject, gesturing for emphasis in a manner quite lacking her former reserve. During an especially flamboyant gesture, her left hand waved past the candle in the centerpiece, and the light caught the diamond ring she wore, making it sparkle so brightly it made Mike's eyes sting. Filled with joy, he swallowed the lump in his throat and draped his arm across the back of Caroline's chair in a gesture of his own.

He took a deep, satisfied breath of the soft summer breeze drifting through a nearby window. The weather had turned suddenly warm these past couple of weeks, and Mike would have bet his badge that the cold part of summer was over at last.

It looks like a charming old building near the Baltimore waterfront, but inside 43 Light Street lurks danger . . . and romance.

Labeled a "true master of intrigue" by *Rave Reviews*, bestselling author Rebecca York continues her exciting series with #213 HOPSCOTCH, coming to you in February.

Paralegal Noel Emery meets an enigmatic man from her past and gets swept away on a thrilling international adventure—where illusion and reality shift like the images in a deadly kaleidoscope. . . .

"Ms. York ruthlessly boggles the brain and then twists our jangled nerves beyond the breaking point in this electrifying foray into hi-tech skullduggery and sizzling romance!"
—Melinda Helfer, *Romantic Times*

Don't miss Harlequin Intrigue #213 HOPSCOTCH!

ROMANCE IS A YEARLONG EVENT!

Celebrate the most romantic day of the year with MY VALENTINE! (February)

CRYSTAL CREEK
When you come for a visit Texas-style, you won't want to leave! (March)

Celebrate the joy, excitement and adjustment that comes with being JUST MARRIED! (April)

Go back in time and discover the West as it was meant to be . . . UNTAMED—Maverick Hearts! (July)

LINGERING SHADOWS
New York Times bestselling author Penny Jordan brings you her latest blockbuster. Don't miss it! (August)

BACK BY POPULAR DEMAND!!!
Calloway Corners, involving stories of four sisters coping with family, business and romance! (September)

FRIENDS, FAMILIES, LOVERS
Join us for these heartwarming love stories that evoke memories of family and friends. (October)

Capture the magic and romance of Christmas past with HARLEQUIN HISTORICAL CHRISTMAS STORIES! (November)

WATCH FOR FURTHER DETAILS IN ALL HARLEQUIN BOOKS!

CALEND